Tony Birch is the author of *Shadowboxing*. His short fiction, poetry, and non-fiction have been published widely. He teaches at the University of Melbourne.

# FATHER'S DAY

## TONY BIRCH

**H**
HUNTER

Hunter Publishers
PO Box 81
Flinders Lane
Melbourne 8009
Australia

www.hunterpublishers.com.au

First published 2009 by Hunter Publishers
Reprinted 2010

Cover design: Design by Committee
Cover photo: Jesse Marlow, www.jessemarlow.com

Printed in Australia by Griffin Press

National Library of Australia
Cataloguing-in-Publication data:

Birch, Tony.
    Father's day / Tony Birch.
    ISBN:9780980517972 (pbk.)
A823.4

For Sara

*My father's house shines hard and bright*
*it stands like a beacon calling me in the night*
*Calling and calling, so cold and alone*
*Shining 'cross this dark highway where our*
*sins lie unatoned.*

— BRUCE SPRINGSTEEN

# CONTENTS

# The Last Time
# I Saw Cherry

My father left the house for the last time during my
second year in high school. He walked out one Sunday
morning after my mother had dragged me down the
road to St Mary's. We usually went to church only at
Christmas and Easter and this was an ordinary dull
Sunday morning in late winter. I guess they must have
agreed to get me out of the house so he could pack up
his stuff and leave without having to say goodbye to me
and embarrass the three of us.

When we got home from church my mother didn't
look a bit surprised to see that our old car, a rusting 1968
Valiant that rarely moved from where it was parked out
front of the house, was gone. When I asked her where
my father had taken the car she ignored the question
and told me to get into the house.

As well as the car, he took his extensive collection of Jazz records with him. Some of them were old 78s and must have weighed a ton. That's why he needed the Valiant, I suppose, to cart them away. We wouldn't miss the records, as they hadn't been played in months anyway. Not since he had hocked the family record player, a three-in-one, and never bothered to redeem it from the pawnshop — even after a big win at the track a few weeks later.

He didn't tell my mother about his win on the horses, of course. My father had never been a man to confess to a full wallet. But she knew he'd won when he came home late that night, half-drunk and dancing a jig around the kitchen, wearing a new sports jacket that he'd bought at the pub.

It wasn't until after tea on the day that he left, as mum and I sat down to watch television, that I noticed the photographs from the wall above the gas heater were also gone. They were of him and his Army mates, and had been taken during his time in National Service, so I guessed he must have taken them with him.

While mum concentrated on the TV, I stared across the room to the brighter squares of wallpaper marking the places where the photographs usually hung. Eventually I stood up, walked across the room, and traced the outline of one of the missing picture frames with a fingertip.

He didn't come home that night, of course. Mum sat me down at the kitchen table the next morning and told me, not that he had left us for good, but just that he would be 'missing' from the house for 'a little while'. Although she made it sound like he was lost, I didn't believe a word of what she was saying.

'How long is a while?' I asked her.

She shrugged her shoulders.

'I don't know, love. Just a while.'

It didn't take long before I discovered that she hadn't told me the full story. I left for school that morning at around the same time the garbage truck worked its way along our street. I opened the front gate just as one of the garbos was picking up our bin. As he emptied its contents into the back of the truck I spotted my father's much younger and still handsome face. He was in his Army uniform, looking out at me from a wooden frame, and was about to be crushed in the mouth of the truck's compactor.

To be perfectly honest I didn't miss him at all in the weeks after he went away. I was used to not seeing that much of him anyway. When his mind wasn't on the horses, the dogs or the trots, my father was a regular at a two-up school in a warehouse down near the docks. Or he spent his time at a late-night card game at a gambling club above a Chinese cafe in the city. He was usually late home of a night and only bothered staggering out of bed before lunchtime if he had a race meeting to get to.

Occasionally, particularly on a Saturday night, he wouldn't creep back home until the early hours of the morning. Sometimes he didn't even beat first-light. And, when he got out of bed for the day, he would put one of his favourite Jazz albums on the record player and lie back on the couch with his music and a cigarette for company, pretty much ignoring my mother and me.

Even as a young boy, I knew that my mother was a lonely woman but she seemed to accept her life without protest. I don't remember them having a single argument in the years they were together. The only disapproving comment I ever heard her utter about him was to casually observe, 'The stranger's home,' when she heard him at the front gate while getting me ready for school one morning.


A few months after he'd walked out my father surprised both of us by turning up at the front gate one Saturday morning. He asked mum if he could take me out for the afternoon. We only got as far as the corner shop for a milkshake that day before he made his way to the local TAB. But he began showing up most Saturdays from then on. Although this irritated her, mum handed me over at the gate with the warning that he had better get me back home by teatime. In exchange for his limited access he would hand her a few dollars; money that she was in desperate need of at the time.

As we walked to the nearby tram stop he would make noises about treating me to the pictures for the afternoon, or even a visit to Luna Park or the Zoo. But we would always end up back at the same TAB, where I would have to hang around while he studied the form guide and placed his bets.

We sometimes moved onto his favourite pub where a lot of handshaking and backslapping went on, after he'd walked into the bar. He was obviously a popular figure. He would order a counter meal for both of us, and a beer for himself and a lemon squash for me. As we sat eating lunch he would give his attention to the radio, cranked to full volume so that the expertise of Bill Collins, the 'voice of racing', could be heard throughout the pub.

Not by accident, my father had a knack of meeting up with a woman during the afternoon. There were lots of different women. They were pretty, and they wore a lot of makeup and perfume that always left me with a headache. They looked nothing like my mother. The women were always years younger than my father but were more than capable of going drink-for-drink with him.

My father had a lot of girlfriends during those visits to the pub but his favourite was Cherry. And she was beautiful.

Cherry had bleached blonde hair that darkened at the roots. She liked to dress in low-cut dresses or blouses and never wore a bra. She also chewed gum and blew bubbles like a schoolgirl. When Cherry first turned up at the hotel she seemed to be on a roster with some of his other girlfriends. Then she started turning up more regularly than the other women. And finally she was the only one.

The first time we met I sat across the table from the two of them as they snuggled into each other like teenagers. When they weren't kissing, Cherry nibbled away at his ear. He would put his hand under the table and Cherry would throw her head back and giggle.

While most other drinkers in the bar sat around in singlets and shorts in summer, or moth-eaten jumpers and stained pants in winter, my father always wore a dark pinstriped suit, clean shirt and tie, along with his 'lucky hat' — the tweed peaked cap that rarely left his head on race days.

I would eventually come to feel guilty about it but it wasn't long before Cherry had won me over. I was madly in love with her. And all it took was an endless supply of lemon squash and potato chips, delivered with pouting smile and generous cleavage. Once she got to know me, Cherry would kiss me goodbye, hard and wet on the lips, before leaving us in the street outside the pub of a Saturday night.

My father seemed to enjoy this as much as I did. He looked on with approval, grinning from ear to ear, as she pressed her lips to mine.

Before dropping me home at night he would remind me, 'Don't mention your girlfriends to your mum; she wouldn't be too happy about it.'

But I was sure that mum knew quite a bit of what was going on without me having to confess a word to her. When I walked into the house of a night, with my clothes reeking of a tell-tale mix of beer, cigarette smoke, and cheap perfume, she would look at me with despair. I knew that I had betrayed her but I couldn't wait to see Cherry again the following weekend.

My father liked to buy Cherry gifts; jewellery, fancy-coloured Sobrani 'cocktail' cigarettes, and bottles of perfume. And he liked to show her off. Whenever they were on the street together passers-by looked at them. I suspect that my father thought that people were staring because they made a handsome couple. I wasn't sure how old Cherry was but anyone could see that she was too young for him.

They began to argue quite a bit; sometimes in the pub, or on the street when he was drunk. Whenever they fought they looked different together, like a father trying to order one of his kids about.

One Saturday morning, after picking me up from the front of the house, my father told me we were going to the races for the day to celebrate their 'first anniversary'. This didn't add up — it had only been six months since he had left the house.

We met Cherry in the city around lunchtime, on the steps under the clocks at Flinders Street Station. Although the intersection in front of us was jammed with racegoers and shoppers, Cherry stood out from the crowd as she crossed the street from Young and Jackson's hotel. She wore a red and white polka dot dress and a black bonnet on her head with a feather stuck in it.

Cherry loved an audience and posed on the steps for us. She asked both of us if we thought she looked French. I thought she looked as beautiful as ever but I said nothing. My father licked his lips, looked her up and down and chuckled, 'Yeah, real French.'

We caught the train to the racetrack and streamed down the gangway leading from the station to the track along with other racegoers. Most of them were dressed like they were about to get married or attend an important court case.

I was surprised by how excited I felt to be at the racetrack. The bookies screamed the race odds at the top of their voices in an attempt to attract punters, while families with picnic baskets and rugs seated along a crowded strip of grass in front of the home straight were already drinking and eating. There was even a brass band playing. And then there were the racehorses.

My father and Cherry left me at the mounting yard and headed for the betting ring. I stood watching as the horses entered in the first race circled a narrow cinder track and was drawn to a barrel-chested grey wearing the number eight saddle cloth. It was the same number I wore playing football for my school team. The horse raised his head and sniffed at the air confidently, before looking over his shoulder as he walked on, guided by his strapper.

I had never been near a horse before, let alone ridden one, but I imagined myself on his back. Not at the racetrack, but 'out on the range' somewhere, as I had seen in so many western movies.

The horses looked so powerful. As I watched them circle the yard for the final time I felt that maybe I understood why my father was drawn to them. Why he talked endlessly about horses and seemed prepared to wager so much money on them. Maybe he just loved them.

I waited in the empty mounting yard until he and Cherry returned to collect me. We managed to squeeze through the crowd and get a good position on the fence, not far off the winning post.

From where we were standing, I couldn't see the horses being guided into the barrier for the first race of the day but I could feel the ripple of anticipation along the fence. The crowd erupted as the line of horses jumped from the gate.

As the roar grew I watched the bright colours of the jockeys' silks bobbing up and down in a cloud of dust along the back straight. I searched the procession of horses for my grey but was unable to distinguish one horse from another.

I could hear and feel the strength of the horses as they entered the home straight. The ground under my feet rumbled. I looked up at my father. He didn't look at all happy. He was grimacing and holding an imaginary pair of reins between clenched fists in front of his face.

He moved the reins desperately back and forward as he urged his horse to the line, 'Nail it here! Nail it! Come on!'

I turned back to the track and caught a glimpse of the number eight saddlecloth as the grey collapsed beneath the jockey. His front legs went first. It was as if he had been tripped by a hidden wire, or spooked by a shadow. As the horse went down the jockey was thrown over his mane and crashed into the turf. The jockey managed to roll to one side, just avoiding the trailing horses about to trample him.

He got his knees and shook his head from side to side. He didn't look to be badly hurt. But the horse was. The animal was lying on his back and making frightful noises that resembled nothing like the neighing and snorting of a horse. I held my hands over my ears to block out a deep, broken cry.

Several track officials ran onto the course. One of them, wearing a red bib with VET stamped across the front, examined the horse. He looked up at the other race officials and glumly shook his head from side to side as he stroked the horse's neck.

The vet stayed with the horse while a small tractor with a large metal tray attached to the front was driven onto the track and manoeuvred alongside the animal. I thought that maybe they were going to try and scoop the horse onto the tray and get it off the track so that it could be taken care of. One of the men began knocking tent poles into the ground with a rubber mallet in a rectangular shape around the animal.

The noise of the crowd fell to a hush when lengths of faded canvas were strung between the poles. With the ends of the canvas drawn together it was no longer possible to see the horse.

My father looked confused. He was gazing at a betting slip, studying it closely, as if it might offer an explanation about what was going on. I looked over at Cherry, who was leaning against the rail. Suddenly, she covered her eyes with one hand and stared down at her red shoes. Other people in the crowd had already turned away from the track and were hurriedly walking away.

I turned back to the track just as a gust of wind lifted the bottom corner of one of the canvas sheets. I could see the vet was standing above the grey. He was holding a dark metal object to the horse's skull. A second official was kneeling on the ground, leaning forward with both palms pressed firmly against the horse's body. The horse raised his head slowly and looked up at the vet.

I heard the dull thud of the bolt gun delivered to the crown of the horse's head, followed by the spasms of its body as it fell back against the rich green grass. The canvas awning fluttered gently in the breeze and then also fell.

Everything around me was quiet except for the rush of air expelled from the horse's lungs and the flapping of canvas in the breeze. The jockey, who had remained on the track, where a St. John's ambulance officer was examining him, dropped to his knees. He lowered his head to his chest.

He suddenly looked like a small boy in a pair of pyjamas, praying at his bedside.

The body of the grey was loaded onto the tractor and covered with one of the sheets of canvas before being driven back along the straight to a far corner of the racecourse behind the mounting yard and stables. By the time the second race of the day came around the crowd had forgotten about the death of the horse. They cheered throughout the next race and went wild with joy as the winning horse passed the post.

I felt sick. I tugged at the sleeve of my father's suit and told him that I didn't want to watch another horse race. He was annoyed but gave me enough money to buy myself lunch and told me to meet him and Cherry at the bottom of the ramp leading up to the train station as soon as the last race was over.

I spent the rest of the afternoon behind one of the grandstands with a few other kids, sliding down a grass embankment on empty cardboard beer boxes. When one of the boys offered me a cigarette I took it and lit up without really thinking about what I was doing. I lay on the grass under the grandstand and had smoked almost half of the cigarette when I started feeling dizzy. I threw it away, rolled onto my side and threw up my lunch.

I had forgotten about the death of the horse until we were back on the train and heading for home, when I was almost certain that I heard the distressed wailing of the injured animal again. I began to sob and, as much as I tried to stop myself from crying, I couldn't stop. My father, who was sitting next to me, tried to ignore me, burying his face in the form guide. An elderly woman sitting alongside Cherry asked him if there was anything she could do to help. Without waiting for an answer from him she leaned across the carriage and offered me a linen handkerchief.

He rested an awkward hand on my shoulder while Cherry stood up from her seat and squeezed herself next to me. When she tried slipping her hand into mine I pulled away from her. The elderly woman looked Cherry up and down disapprovingly while tut-tutting under her breath.

My father tapped me on the shoulder and said, 'It's nothing, it's nothing,' more to himself than to me. He was wrong, of course. I looked up at him. In that moment I hated him. I wanted to scream. I wished I were a man, and a bigger man than him, so I could punch him in the face.

Other people in the carriage were looking at us, which further annoyed and embarrassed my father. When it became obvious that his attempts to pacify me were having no impact he got angry. He let his arm slip from my shoulder and gave me a sharp nudge in the ribs with his elbow. The blow momentarily winded me. And it did stop me from crying but only because I could hardly breathe.

'Stop carrying on like a baby,' he yelled. 'How do you reckon I feel? I had twenty dollars each way on that horse, and I've lost the fucking lot. So you stop all your blubbering like a sook. No fucking more!'

I had never heard him talk that way before. It hurt me a lot more than the poke in the ribs.

Cherry began to growl. She leaned across my body

so she could get to him. As she waved a finger in his face I looked down the front of her dress at her breasts as they shook from side to side. Right then I forgot about the horse and my father's anger.

'Leave him alone. He's just a kid. A poor kid. That was awful, what happened to the horse, back there. Who cares about the money? Bugger your twenty dollars.'

I was sure that he was about to yell at her as well, but he didn't. He jumped up from his seat and moved to the far side of the carriage. He was sulking like a big kid. Cherry also got up. She lit a cigarette and started pacing up and down the aisle between the seats. Each time she turned around to face him she would give my father a filthy look.

I slumped the back of my head against the headrest and closed my eyes.

I woke to the sound of the train whistle announcing our return to the city. My body rocked gently from side to side and I could feel something comforting resting against my shoulder. When I opened my eyes the elderly woman who had been sitting across from us was gone. My father hadn't moved from his seat in the corner. He was brooding with his chin on his hand staring out of the train window into the empty rail yards.

When I realised I was nestled into Cherry's breasts I closed my eyes again and allowed her scent to fill my nostrils. I did not move until I felt her breath against my cheek a few minutes later when she whispered, 'Here we are, home.'

As we waited for the crowd to empty from the train carriage I picked up the crumpled form guide from the seat next to mine. It was open at race one. A heavy black line had been drawn through the name of horse number eight, blotting it out.

When we got off the train Cherry kissed me on the cheek and walked away from us without as much as a glance at my father. We both watched as she headed up the ramp and her red, high-heeled shoes gradually disappeared from view.

That was the last time I saw Cherry. And a few months later, I would see my father for the last time too.

# The Day of the Hen

What Sonny Macris offered as a choice, when I'd spoken to him on the phone earlier that morning, I understood much more clearly as an ultimatum. That was a problem I'd always had with Sonny. He rarely said what he meant, although occasionally he said exactly what he meant. Knowing which was which was important to your state of wellbeing. Get the money I owed to him by six that night, he'd reminded me more than once, or I'd be getting a visitor.

I was told to drop the money off at the suburban café, where he kept a more-or-less legitimate take-away out the front, while running a highly lucrative card game from the back door. I knew the establishment well enough and it was not a place I had fond memories of, having lost a brick there more than once. One time too many, as it had turned out. When I got to the café I was to ask for one of his heavies, an ex-shearer by the name of Dennis. I was to leave the money with him.

Four hundred dollars was hardly an amount of money that Sonny would normally bother chasing himself. It was little more than small change, really. But collecting it had become a matter of principle, he'd made a point of reminding me, more than once, over the telephone.

It wasn't just the conviction in his voice, on the other end of the line, that persuaded me to take the threat seriously. I'd previously seen the results of Sonny's handiwork and it was ugly. He had a habit of insisting that accumulated interest on a debt be paid for in pain and suffering.

Sonny was particularly unhappy that I had been seen out and about at a nightclub the week before, splashing around my winnings from a bet I'd made on a middleweight title bout. It happened to be a nightclub that he had an interest in and one where enough loose-mouthed patrons knew I was in his debt. They couldn't wait to crawl back to Sonny and report my misdemeanour to him.

I left the house around eight that morning with a sense of urgency. I had a lot of running around to do and no wheels to get me from A to B or beyond. I'd been driving a '76 Charger around for a few months but had sold it back to the yard at less than half the price I paid for it, when I was desperate to get my hands on some cash in a hurry. It was cash that I should have passed on to Sonny to clear the ledger but unfortunately I got waylaid, found myself at another big card game and walked out with nothing.

Getting my hands on the money didn't turn out to be as difficult as I'd expected and I managed to scrounge the lot by four o'clock that afternoon. I got off to a great start by collecting on a hundred dollar debt that Latimer, my neighbour from three doors down the street, had owed me for weeks. I didn't heavy him. I'm not like that. I pleaded with tears and tales of broken thumbs.

Latimer had knocked at my door one Thursday morning and more-or-less begged the money out of me, telling me he was broke and desperate to get his hands on the cash for an ampoule of super juice that he could spike his greyhound with.

The dog went by the name of Flashdance, which was a misnomer, if there's ever been one. It was set to run in the fifth race at Sandown that night. Latimer was sure that she would need some extra pep in her step if she was to get anywhere near the bunny. He outlined his scheme with such enthusiasm that I not only lent him the hundred, I handed over another fifty to put on the dog for me.

The plan turned out to be a total fuck-up. I don't know what vet Latimer used for the dope but I wouldn't send my mum's budgie to him for as much as a check-up. I'd held the dog down while Latimer injected her. Then he put her in the car and drove across town to the track. When he got there she was laid out across the back seat, sleeping like a baby. Latimer couldn't rouse her at all and Flashdance didn't come good until around lunchtime the next day. She hasn't run a race since.

I also picked up an advance of two hundred and fifty dollars from a milk bar owner in Richmond who I regularly supply with a delivery of 'tax-free' cigarettes. The only catch being I had to throw in a couple of extra cartons with my next drop, a reasonable price to pay, I thought, considering his financial risk.

I negotiated the final fifty with a pawnbroker in Russell Street over a watch I had been holding for a colleague in the trade. It would have been worth twice that on the street but I didn't have the time to tout around the pubs for a buyer. As soon as I passed the watch across the glass-top counter I knew I would have some serious explaining to do later on but this was not the time to think about it, as I had a more pressing issue to deal with. I headed for Flinders Street Station with the four hundred dollars stuffed into one of my socks.

The last words Sonny had said to me before slamming the phone down in my ear was, 'Don't be fucking late, son, don't be late.' He said it slowly and very quietly, in his distinctive gravelled voice, but his words came down the line like the screech of a demented chainsaw mixed with the violence of a barking mad pit bull.

It wasn't until I reached the station that I realised I didn't have the additional three dollars and seventy cents I needed for the train ticket. I could see that the ticket stalls leading to the platforms were all manned, not only by regular station attendants, but an army of railway police, suited up, badged and eager to grab anyone who didn't have a ticket.

I looked up at the timetable. I had just three minutes to get on the next train for St. Albans if I was to meet Sonny's deadline. But I also had a more immediate problem to deal with. The automatic ticketing machines do not accept fifty-dollar notes and the queue snaking away from the only open ticket box was going nowhere.

Even if I'd had the time to buy a ticket, Sonny would not be happy with me pulling up short. The amount would be an insult, likely to upset him more than if I were, say, fifty dollars light, which would at least be a sum worthy of negotiation. Three dollars and a miserable seventy cents would be understood for what it was, a mark of disrespect.

As I wrestled with my limited options, I was saved by a teenage kid wearing a baseball cap and expensive sneakers, who at that moment decided to take a suicidal run at the one of the stalls, straddle it and duck and weave around the patrolling attendants on the other side.

The kid hurdled the gate with room to spare but landed awkwardly and slipped on the tiled concourse. He was quickly set upon by half a dozen railway police. As he was being slammed into the tiles for the third time I slipped through the now unmanned gate and walked calmly down the ramp to my train, just as the station attendant announced that we were leaving.

The train was crowded, mostly with teenagers in school uniform. At North Melbourne station the first factory workers, who had just knocked off for the day, joined us. I would have found a seat had I been quick enough but I was preoccupied with thoughts of the train breaking down between stations and me not getting to the café in time. I imagined the disappointed Sonny at a table in a back corner of the smoky room amusing himself with a set of bolt cutters.

I shouldn't have worried myself sick over being just a few minutes late. It's the money that counts, right? But seeing as Sonny had never been the predictable type, nor entirely reasonable, I had no idea what he might do if I was late.

Sonny had some nasty habits. One of them was that he liked to make an example of anyone guilty of untidiness or disrespect. 'Incentive tales,' Sonny liked to call the stories he told about those who had abused his generosity in the past. Whether they were true or not, his clientele, his business partners, and sworn enemies alike had all heard stories, such as the one about his car boot being permanently lined with black plastic and the supply of gaffer tape, a shovel, and the box of crude tools of the trade that he kept on hand.

We crossed the river and pulled in at Footscray Station and, although the carriage was already full, more schoolkids and afternoon market shoppers forced their way onto the train, along with their bags and makeshift trolleys stuffed full with fruit and vegetables and meats.

By the time more factory workers got on at Tottenham we were packed in like sheep on our way to the slaughterhouse, with every square foot of the carriage occupied. Luckily, when we pulled in at Sunshine, around half of the passengers got off the train. I quickly grabbed a seat before anyone could take it from me.

I was sitting next to a bloke wearing a dirty boilersuit. Looking at him, covered in grease from head to foot, half asleep and worn out by hard work, I was reminded of the many reasons I had managed to shy away from a proper job for all these years.

An old man struggled onto the train just as the doors were closing. He was pushing an old pram jammed full with crushed aluminium cans. He also had a heavy canvas bag under one arm. It was overflowing with crushed cans. He offloaded the bag and dragged it across the floor with him as he guided the pram with the other hand, crashing into punters as he did. It was only when he stopped in front of my seat that I noticed he also had a bird with him. It was in a cage balanced on top of the pram.

It was a beautiful looking hen.

The bird tilted its head to one side and looked out through the wire, directly at the factory worker sitting next to me. He stared back at the bird as he nudged me in the ribs.

'What do you reckon it is? Is it a rooster or what?'

To be honest I don't know a lot about birds, let alone the poultry family. The bird was no rooster but, after looking at it a second time, I realised that it was no ordinary hen, either. Its feathers were a rich brown and it had a white speckled necklace of feathers around its neck.

I leaned forward so that I could study the bird more closely. I tapped on the wire frame of the cage to get its attention. Whether it was the cage it was cooped up in, or maybe the crowd gathering around it, the bird was clearly unhappy.

'I dunno mate. I'm not sure what it is but it's not a rooster. It hasn't got one of those things on its head. You know, those red things. Its most likely some sort of chicken.'

He sat up a little straighter so that he could give the bird his full attention.

'You're right. It's not a rooster but its no chicken either. Can't be. A chicken's just a baby bird, isn't it? This is fully grown.'

And then he added, almost as an afterthought, 'But it's not only roosters that have that red thing on their head.'

He made a 'click click' sound with his tongue, trying to catch the attention of the bird. It was a poor attempt at any sort of birdsong. The hen turned her back on him in disgust.

'What do you think it does then, the bird?' he asked.

I had no idea what he meant but then I didn't really give a fuck. I was still worrying about what Sonny might do to me if I was late.

'What do you mean, mate, what does it do?'

'The bird. What does it do? You know, some birds can talk. Others have a nice whistle. I had a mate who used to live in a block of flats in Yarraville. And he used to have a cockatoo, this pet cocky that used to fly down to the clothesline from the balcony and thieve all the pegs from the line and bring them back to him. And not his pegs. Never. Only knocked off the pegs that belonged to the other tenants.'

I watched the bird in the cage while he told his story of the cockatoo. I didn't say so but the story sounded like bullshit to me. Any cockatoo that could fly down to the clothesline could also fly away from a miserable life in a block of flats in Yarraville. I was sure that it would have headed for the nearest gum tree with its first opportunity for freedom, unless it was some type of homing cocky and I was confident that there was no such breed.

I leaned over and tapped at the wire again. Although the old man gave me a look of discouragement I kept on knocking anyway.

'It lays eggs, I suppose. That's why people keep them, isn't it?'

Maybe it was a fighting bird, I thought. If it were, there'd be a bout on somewhere. A bout with a lot of money wagered. I started to think about the four hundred tucked into my sock before coming to my senses. I pointed to the bird's owner, who had been listening to our conversation but had not said a word. 'Ask him, why don't ya?'

'The bird, mate? You've just bought the fella, have you? At the market?'

The old man looked a little offended that his hen might be a mere market bird.

'She's not a fella, mate. And I've had her for years.'

He put a finger through the wire. As he did so the bird moved across the cage and let the man gently stroke her neck as he whispered to her, 'Maggie, my baby girl, Maggie.'

'Why's she on the train with you?' the factory worker asked. 'You moving house or something?'

'No. I've been out doing me work.'

He grabbed the handle of the canvas bag and shook it like mad. The rattling of cans could be heard the length of the carriage.

'She don't like staying at home on her own since the telly broke down. She gets all anxious if I leave her on her own for too long.'

If the other passengers weren't upset enough about the precious space taken up by the hen and the old man's collection of scrap metal, they were really pissed off when the bird suddenly moved to the back of the cage and, in one swift movement, stuck its beak through the wire and pecked viciously at the bodies now pressing against the side of the cage.

A piercing scream actually shook the carriage windows when the bird stabbed its beak into a schoolgirl's fleshy thigh. Several of her friends joined her in a series of high-pitched squeals of their own, sending the poor bird into greater panic. Having been locked away, myself, on more than one occasion, I had a fair idea how the bird was feeling.

A woman aged somewhere in her late sixties, sporting a B52 hairdo and carrying an old-fashioned string bag bursting with oranges, was knocked off her feet by the retreating crowd. As she landed on top of me she winked, 'It's your lucky day, love,' before struggling to her feet again.

The bird started knocking its head against the top of the cage. The worried old man lifted the lid a little to give it some room. My companion waved a warning hand towards the old man.

'Wouldn't do that if I were you mate. Wouldn't do that.'

But it was too late. As the old man lifted the lid of the cage the bird escaped and flew into the air. He lunged forward and tried to grab hold of it. He wasn't quick enough. She frantically flapped her wings about and fly-hopped her way to the other end of the carriage, briefly touching down on the bald scalp of a middle-aged man, then the gelled flattop of a teenage boy, and finally the head of a pig-tailed schoolgirl.

As passengers joined in the chase the bird made her way back to our end of the carriage. She eventually perched herself on the luggage rack above my seat. My weary worker friend looked up at the bird, pointed to it and put his finger to his lips.

'Shhh.'

As the carriage went quiet with anticipation he leapt from his seat and grabbed the bird in both hands — just for a moment. Maybe it was the grease and oil all over his hands? Just when I was sure he had secured her, the bird slipped out of his grasp, flew into the air again and disappeared into the crowd.

Bodies spread and feathers flew. Somehow the bird popped into the air again. I was just as shocked as the bird herself when she suddenly landed in my lap. Instinctively, I wrapped my arms around her and held on as tight as I could. As I felt the bird gradually calm down I relaxed my grip on her neck, worried that I might choke her to death.

The crowd parted. The old man walked towards me. As I passed the bird to him he whispered, 'Thank you'.

He looked a little embarrassed about the scene Maggie had just caused. Then he bowed his head and actually kissed her on the neck, whispering something to her before returning her to the security of the cage.

The train pulled into St. Albans station. I looked down at my watch. I had just a few minutes to spare. I filed out of the train behind the old man and the bird. She craned her neck and stared at me from the cage. Was it a look of gratitude for rescuing her from the crowd, or was the bird angry that I was responsible for her being incarcerated for a second time? I couldn't really say. I don't know birds that well.

I searched the length of the platform. I didn't want to risk being caught without a ticket. My escape route would be to jump down from the platform and cross the tracks at the far end of the station, where I could hurdle a low cyclone-wire fence and cross an empty paddock to the main street and the café.

It wasn't until I was about to hop down from the platform that I noticed there was no station attendant on duty to collect the tickets. I could have simply walked out through the gate with the other passengers but, as I was already on my way, I kept going.

It was the one mistake that I made that day.

As I jumped the fence I noticed two men approaching me. One of them was a little shorter than me and built like a welterweight, lean and all muscle. The other one was heavier-built and clumsy looking. He was at least half a foot taller than me and twice as wide.

It looked as if Sonny had sent a forward posse to escort me to the café; unnecessary, I thought to myself. I had to admit that it was a good piece of theatre for a suburban gangster trying to create an impression for the bigger boys from the inner city. I was sure I was in real trouble when the taller of the two men reached into his back pocket.

'Fuck,' I whispered, 'not a gun?' All because of a lazy

four hundred dollars?

'Stop there. Transit Authority,' he called, as he pulled a badge from his pocket and stuck it in my face. 'Do you have a valid ticket for travel on this train?'

I thought it best to plead ignorance.

'Sorry? A ticket?'

'Yeah, a ticket. Are you deaf or what? Your ticket. Don't tell me, you haven't got one? You can't travel on a train for free. We're not in Communist Russia.'

His offsider felt an immediate need to correct him.

'There is no Communist Russia, Dave. There hasn't been for a few years now. They're a market economy these days, the Russians. They've got more billionaires per head of population that anywhere in Europe.'

Dave ignored him.

'You got ID on you?'

I looked down at my watch. I had about one minute to spare if I was to get to the café on time. I wasn't sure what to do. If I tried to run I might get past Dave but his athletically built deputy would grab me for sure.

As I contemplated the embarrassment of getting done for the major crime of fare evasion I could hear a strange combination of squeaking and rattling and squawking heading in our direction. It was the old man and his pram, loaded with his treasure trove of crushed cans and one very angry bird.

She obviously remained unhappy about the incident on the train.

The old man stopped on the footpath, parked the pram and bird, and walked across the paddock. The further away he got from her, the louder she squawked. She was obviously a pet that fretted for her owner. She would have sent the neighbours crazy if he'd left her at home on her own when he went out collecting cans.

As he walked toward me, I saw that the old man was holding something in his hand. He waved it at me.

'Your ticket, son. You dropped your ticket on the platform.' He was desperate for me to take it.

'Your ticket. You lost it back there.'

It took a moment for me to understand that he was trying to save me but, when it finally clicked, I grabbed the ticket out of his hand.

'Thankyou. That's real considerate of you, mate.'

I studied the ticket like the foreign object it was before handing it to over to Officer Dave.

'This is what you want, is it? My train ticket.'

Dave looked doubtful. He poked an accusing finger in the direction of the old man.

'His ticket? You sure? Where's your own ticket, then?'

The old man nodded over his shoulder.

'Back there, in the bin at the station. I don't like to litter.'

Officer Dave sniffed at the air, trying to locate the rat he could smell. The old man turned around and trundled back to his pram. He picked up his canvas bag, slung it over his shoulder, and continued pushing the pram along the footpath. The hen poked its beak through the wire and continued her complaint to the world.

While Dave inspected my ticket his mate watched as the old man and the bird toddled away.

'Hey Dave. Did you see that bird the old fella's got with him? I've seen a lot of chickens before. My brother used to run an egg farm out the back of Laverton, but, fuck, I've never seen a chicken like that before.'

By the time Dave had looked up from my ticket the old man and the bird had disappeared around the corner.

'It wasn't no chicken. By the sound of it, it was an adult bird, for sure. All baby birds are chickens. A chicken is not a breed, Charlie. A chicken is just a fucking chicken.'

I tapped the toe of my right shoe against my left ankle, checking that the roll of money was where I had planted it. I looked down at my watch and thought about Sonny. If I were lucky he'd be at the card table, sitting on a bet and a good hand, and would have forgotten about me. If not, he'd be standing at the back door, shifting from foot to foot.

# Gardening for Pleasure

There is an elderly woman who lives in the pink weatherboard house a little further down the street from here and whenever I see her she says hello to me. She introduced herself one morning as we were standing at the traffic lights together. I was waiting to cross the street into the park that I walk through each morning on my way to the public library.

I'm not sure where the woman from the pink house was heading to that morning but she was carrying a shopping bag, so I suppose she was going to the shops. As we waited for the lights to change she looked across at me and smiled.

'You're from the halfway house, aren't you?' she said.

'The halfway house.' I liked the way it sounded, although I wasn't quite sure what she meant by it. Halfway to where, I wondered?

I've been in this house for around eighteen months. Before that, I was in the hospital for several years; more years than I can remember. My family had always referred to it simply as 'the hospital' although, if you look it up in the telephone book, you'll find that it's not just a hospital, but a 'mental hospital'.

Nobody in my family would dare whisper the word mental.

If that word isn't bad enough, when I was reading through some old maps in the reference section of the library one morning, I discovered that the hospital was originally known as a 'lunatic asylum'. When I saw those words on the map even I conjured up images of crazy people in straight jackets.

During my last year, or so, at the hospital we were allowed to walk down the road to a nearby hotel each Thursday night, where we would play a few games of pool and drink glasses of beer. I enjoyed those nights, a few hours of freedom once a week, when we could simply be ourselves, rather than patients or inmates, as we were called in the bad old days before we came to be known as residents and clients.

Before we went into the hotel for the first time, we held an impromptu meeting in the car park. We decided that, once we were inside, we wouldn't talk about our lives at the hospital at all. We didn't want the other patrons becoming suspicious about where we came from.

Our plan fell through immediately. The young man

behind the bar, pulling the beers and wiping down the tables with a soggy towel, took a good look at us, as we stood nervously at the bar. He leaned across to me, put his hand out for me to shake it and said, 'You blokes must be from the nuthouse up the road.'

Just like that, he said it. I am sure he meant no offence and none was taken.

Over the following months we visited the hotel each week. We were treated like any of the customers as long as we obeyed the rules of the bar:

DO NOT ASK FOR CREDIT

DO NOT BET ON GAMES OF POOL

and

DO NOT SMOKE OVER THE POOL TABLE

I sometimes miss those nights at the pub and the men from the hospital I became friends with. Occasionally I see one of them, Carlo, walking around the city. I used to say hello to him but he doesn't seem to remember me. Like me, he now has his freedom but not much else. When the hospital closed down and we were 'deinstitutionalised' we were told that we would be much happier, as we would become part of the community. But it hasn't quite worked out that way, if you want my opinion.

We each have our own room here at the house, out of respect for our privacy and independence, we are told. I have to say, I like the sanctuary of my own little room. In the hospital we slept in open wards and there were no doors on either the shower cubicles or the toilets. I was sitting on the toilet one morning and I noticed some marks in the doorframe where hinges must once have been. I asked one of the attendants why the toilet doors had been taken away.

'For your own welfare,' he answered lazily, as he shrugged his shoulders.

I'm sure he didn't believe what he'd said, any more than I did.

Having my own room here does protect my privacy but I don't stay inside for longer than I need to. I like to get out early of a morning and go for a walk, visit the library or sit in the park and feed the birds with the crusts left over from breakfast. The house cook, Maria, who arrives early each week-morning, gathers the crusts for me in a plastic bag.

Some of the other residents rarely leave their rooms and nobody seems to care, or even take much notice. You could be dead for days before anyone would realise there was something wrong.

When Martha, who has a room two doors along the corridor, first arrived here she behaved just like that. She rarely came out, except to go to the bathroom of a morning for a shower. As she never joined us for meals in the dining room, I began to worry that she wasn't eating properly. When I walked past her door in the morning I could smell burnt toast, so I knew that she was eating *something*. But who can survive on toast?

We're not supposed to cook or eat in our bedrooms anyway but we tend to get away with it. 'Independent Living', as a brochure left on a table in the hallway explains, means that government bureaucrats come to the house only once a month on inspection visits. We do have residential workers here but they have more pressing issues to deal with than the welfare of residents, such as searching the house for the furniture that is always disappearing from the common room.

In more recent months the workers have also been dealing with the problem of stray cats turning up in the backyard. None of the residents have been prepared to own up to bringing them home from the laneway behind the house and feeding them but someone from the house is leaving the saucers of milk and opened tins of plain label cat food in the yard.

A notice went up in the dining room to discourage whoever has been feeding them. In addition to reminding us that it was a house rule not to leave food out for the cats, we were warned that THEY SPREAD DISEASE.

A few mornings later a ginger cat that I had seen around the yard turned up dead on the backdoor mat. The animal was all floppy and I think its neck had been broken. Several of us saw it when we came downstairs for breakfast. I wasn't sure if the notice in the dining room and the dead cat were connected — but if the murder of the cat was supposed to be a warning to the other strays, it didn't work, as they kept on coming into the garden.

When Martha did venture out of her room she didn't speak to anyone beyond the briefest 'hello'. She began to spend a lot of time in the garden, sitting by herself in a cane chair and catching the morning sun. We always referred to the yard as the garden but, before Martha arrived, it was little more than a patch of weed-infested grass outside the back door. It was littered with cigarette butts and lolly wrappers, as was the narrow strip of bare ground on each side of the paved courtyard that runs down to the iron gates where the yard meets the bluestone laneway behind the house.

While I was shaving in the upstairs bathroom one morning I heard the sound of a shovel digging in the dirt outside my window. I opened the window and looked down into the yard. I could see Martha turning the soil over in one of the beds of tired soil. She kneeled down and combed through the bed with her bare hands, pulling the weeds up and tossing them over her shoulder as she worked her way along the fence.

Over the following weeks she brought punnets of seedlings home from the hardware store, annuals and vegetables mostly. Martha worked the soil each morning and watered the seedlings, before returning to her room. It wasn't too long before the beds were a splash of colour; of petunias and begonias. Just as quickly the rusting fences were draped in a tangle of tomato vines, sweet pea, and broad beans.

One morning Martha dragged a kid's plastic sandpit into the garden from the laneway, where it had been dumped. The pool was shaped like a giant shell. I watched from the dining room as Martha dug a deep hole in the garden bed and laid the shell in it. She then lined the edge of the shell with some broken bricks and rocks that had been lying in a back corner of the yard. I didn't realise until she began filling the shell with water from the garden hose that Martha had built a pond for us.

Whenever I looked out of the bathroom window to the garden, Martha would be down there working. From my first floor vantage point I could also see into the dining room, where Trevor, one of the residential workers, sat in his chair after breakfast had ended and the tables had been cleared away. Most of the workers treated us well and did their jobs professionally. Trevor did not. He thought nothing of bursting into our rooms unannounced, particularly when he knew that the women were getting dressed in the morning.

One morning, Albie, who had the room between Martha and I, confided that he was convinced that it was Trevor who had killed the ginger cat.

'Are you sure?' I asked, surprised and a little fearful.

'I'm certain.'

'Did you see him do it?' That would have been terrifying.'

Albie put a hand on my shoulder.

'No, I didn't see anything. But it was him, for sure. Next time you see him take a good look at his eyes and then try telling me he's not a killer.'

While Albie had suggested that I get close enough to take a good look in his eyes, whenever Trevor walked by us he warned me to, 'Steer wide of that one, steer wide.' I was sure that it was Albie who was feeding the cats. No one had actually seen him do it but Albie had been spending a lot of time in the yard petting the cats and talking to them.

Although he was supposed to be working, Trevor would sit in his chair for most of the morning, reading the paper while occasionally looking out to the garden and watching Martha as she worked. He would wait until she had gone from the house for the day before getting up from his chair and strolling into the back yard. Then he would light a cigarette and take a couple of puffs on it while he looked around to see if he was being watched. If no one was looking, he would piss all over Martha's garden beds, chuckling to himself, before throwing his butt into the pond. Sometimes, he pissed in there as well.

As I watched him from my window, I wanted to run downstairs and yell at him to stop. But I never did. I didn't have the courage to confront him. None of us did. Trevor knew as much and our cowardice only encouraged him to bully us more.

I was surprised to see Martha at the library one afternoon. We found ourselves in the same line at the loans desk. When she noticed that I was looking at her she quickly turned the other way. We cautiously turned back to each other, settling long enough to say hello. I suddenly became nervous and could wait no longer for the line to progress, so I dropped the books that I'd intended to borrow on the nearest shelf and quickly walked out of the library.

It wasn't much of a meeting, that first afternoon. But after that day, whenever I passed Martha in the hallway at the house, or in the park, or increasingly at the library, we did say hello to each other, although we were not quite ready to stop and talk at length. After a few weeks Martha introduced a half wave of her hand into our brief exchanges. I tried doing the same, with no real fluency, so I stopped waving altogether.

If Martha was aware that Trevor was urinating on her vegetables and using the garden bed as an ashtray, she didn't mention it to anyone. She continued to patiently tend her vegetables and flowers each morning and tidy any mess he had left. The plants looked remarkably healthy and didn't appear to suffer at all as a result of Trevor's vandalism. Maybe that is what motivated him to shift to a more destructive phase?

One night after dinnertime Trevor had just arrived at the house for a night shift. He was quite drunk. When I passed him in the hallway he scowled at me before staggering on. Later that night I was in bed reading when I heard a racket in the yard. I got out of bed, walked across the hallway to the bathroom and looked out of the window. It was Trevor. He was kicking over the rubbish bins. He looked around the yard before he started stomping on the garden beds and ripping vegetables and flowers out of the ground.

The next morning I looked out of the bathroom window to see Martha crawling around on her hands and knees, retrieving as many of her plants as possible and returning them to the ground. The water in the pond was ink-black. It had been filled with dirt.

I stopped shaving, dressed as quickly as I could, and ran downstairs to help her. I searched around the patch of ground where Trevor had thrown the annuals. The bright mauves and crimsons of the petunias made them easy to spot. I handed the plants to Martha, who didn't say a word about what had happened as she carefully replanted the seedlings in the ground before filling the watering can.

Two of the stray cats were sniffing around in the garden bed beneath the spot where a tomato vine had been ripped away from the fence. When I walked over to repair the vine I saw a black kitten lying on the ground. It was dead. One of the adult cats, perhaps sensing death in the air, looked around with fear before scaling the tin fence. The other cat, which may have been the kitten's mother, sat next to its limp body and did not move.

I was too afraid to bend down and pick the kitten up. When Martha saw what I was staring at she picked up her shovel and dug a hole. She gently picked the kitten up and put it in the ground. The adult cat sat next to the hole and looked down at the kitten as Martha began filling it with dirt. When she had finished she placed two bricks on top of the grave.

'If we don't do this the mother cat might come along and dig up her baby. I've seen it happen before, when I was a child.'

Martha stood in front of the grave that she had just made and mumbled a few words to herself as the adult cat sat between her feet. I think she may have been praying.

When we had finished repairing the garden bed we refreshed the pond with clean water and then washed our hands at the sink in the kitchen. Martha asked if I would like to share a pot of tea with her. We sat on one of the benches outside the door leading to the dining room. She asked me if I wanted sugar in my tea. Although I said, 'No, thank you,' the strong mug of brew in my hand tasted very sweet.

'I'm sorry about the garden,' I said. 'You've done a lot of work. All of us here, we really appreciate it. Except for ... Trevor, of course.' I pointed to the garden bed. 'He did this.'

Martha was not surprised.

'I know.' She nodded in the direction of the plants. 'It's all right. They will survive.' She looked along the garden bed towards the back fence. 'But not the cats, if we let this go on.'

The next time I saw Martha at the library she had another book under her arm, *Gardening For Pleasure*. We sat down at one of the tables and had a long conversation — about vegetables mostly. She listed the plants she would grow if she had her own garden; ones that she would not have to abandon, as there would be no need to move on when she was better.

Martha's wish was for a bigger garden plot, she explained to me. It would be a place where she could plant all her favourite vegetables — eggplant, capsicums, potatoes and sprouts. I don't like sprouts at all, so I told her so.

'Are there vegetables that you don't like, that you wouldn't plant?'

'Definitely,' she laughed. 'When I was a kid my father hated waste, and we couldn't leave the table until we'd eaten everything on the plate. I didn't like swede or cauliflower. Parsnip neither. Just the smell of it made me gag. But he made me eat the lot.'

She looked sad for a moment before going on.

What's your favourite vegetable?'

'Sweet potato.'

'Good choice. Maybe we'll plant some.'

She looked down at my hands as they wrapped themselves protectively around a colour plate edition of *Birds of Australia*.

'You love your books, don't you?'

I looked around the room, noticing the late summer light hugging the windows. I brushed my fingertips across the front cover of the book.

'Yes, I love books. I always have.'

I felt comfortable with Martha until she asked about my family. I think she was more embarrassed than me when I began to stutter nervously.

'I'm sorry. I shouldn't have asked. It's not my business,' she said.

We sat in the quiet of the library for several minutes. I didn't want our conversation to end so awkwardly but I had no idea what I could say to break the silence. Neither did she, so we said nothing. A little later, as we walked home through the park together, I invited her to have a meal with us in the dining room that night.

'Maria, our cook, she does wonderful meals. You don't have to talk if you don't feel up to it. The others, I know they would like to tell you how much they are enjoying the garden.'

She did have dinner with us that night and we all enjoyed it. Afterwards, I walked upstairs to my room feeling happy about how the day had gone. I felt good, until I saw Trevor waiting for me at the top of the stairs. He had just come on duty for the night. He was drunk again.

I tried to walk around him but he would not let me pass by.

'Where do think you're going?' he barked at me.

I pointed to the bathroom door.

'Just to the toilet, before I go to bed.'

'The toilet? Bullshit. You're never out of the

bathroom. In there all the time, whacking off. I bet. You dirty old man.'

He started chuckling uncontrollably.

'You fucking nutters are all the same, playing with yourselves all the time.'

I ignored what he said. It wasn't as if I hadn't heard it before.

'Excuse me, I need to use the toilet,' I said as firmly as I could as I brushed by him.

I was woken again in the night by the now familiar banging of rubbish bins. When I sat up in bed I could hear the screeching cries of a cat. It was obviously in pain. I put my dressing gown on and went into the hallway. Albie was just coming out of the bathroom where he had been looking out of the window.

'It's Trevor. He's down there again,' he said, pointing down the stairway. 'Can you hear the poor baby kittens? He's going to kill them all if we don't do something. He's a murderer. A murderer.'

Albie looked as if he was about to burst into tears.

We both turned around when we heard footsteps a little further along the hallway. It was Martha. When she saw Albie and I standing in the darkened hallway she defensively gripped the front of her dressing gown. We heard another cry of a cat and then Trevor, screaming and cursing to himself.

Martha walked past us to the top of the stairway. 'You're right, Albie. We have to do something to stop him.'

As Albie and I tentatively followed her down the stairs, I wondered what it was that we could actually do to stop Trevor. I could think of nothing.

We crept into the dining room. The sliding door leading into the garden was open. We could see Trevor stomping through the vegetable patch outside the sliding glass door. He was laughing wildly and hooting to the full moon as he kicked plants and dirt into the air.

'That man is a serious mental case,' Albie observed as we looked across the room in horror.

The three of us heard the sickening dull thud as Trevor's head slammed into one of the rocks edging Martha's pond. One moment he was wildly enjoying himself and the next he had slipped and fallen heavily. I could see the outline of his body in the moonlight, laid out across the garden bed amongst the flowers. Trevor wasn't moving.

We waited for a few minutes before Albie and I followed Martha across the room to the doorway leading out to the garden. Trevor was lying face down in the pond, with most of his head submerged. He looked remarkably peaceful for such a violent man.

As the three of us stood frozen to the spot, unable to say a word, the cat that had kept vigil over the dead kitten jumped down from the side fence and walked across the yard to where Trevor was lying. It began sniffing at his muddy boots before working its way along one leg until it reached Trevor's outstretched hand, which was clutching a head of flowers. The cat sniffed tentatively at

Trevor's hand before sticking out its tongue and gently licking it.

Martha walked out into the garden and looked down at the cat. She bent forward and stroked its neck as the cat began to nibble at the tips of Trevor's fingers. The cat put its nose in the air, sniffed a couple of times and contentedly strolled away.

I turned to Albie. He had his hands buried in the pockets of his dressing gown as he watched Martha and the cat.

'Hey Albie, what should we do now?' I asked. 'Shouldn't we ring for an ambulance or something?'

He took a hand out of his pocket and rested it on my shoulder.

'Yeah. In a minute. In a minute. Just let me get my breath back.'

# Cartography

There were just the two empty seats on the bus; one behind the driver where a handwritten notice marked TEACHER had been placed, and another down the back, near the exit door. The driver was already warning the kids that they would have to behave themselves. Most were too excited to keep either still or quiet. They were jumping up and down on the seats and calling out to each other across the aisle. They ignored their parents standing on the footpath until the bus pulled away from the kerb, when they broke into a cheer, stamped their feet and waved back excitedly.

We were not yet out of the street before a group of girls, who had earlier commandeered the backseat, began belting out the first lines of a familiar pop song. They had an extensive repertoire and didn't let up until we arrived at our destination a little over a half hour later.

TONY BIRCH

A week or so earlier my nine-year-old daughter, Meg, had asked me if I would like to accompany her class on their excursion to the new state museum. I wasn't keen on the idea when she surprised me with it over the tea table but hadn't been quick enough with an excuse that might have got me off the hook.

I had been given the lofty title of 'Parent—Helper' for the day. When I joined in the line to get onto the bus Meg's Year Four teacher, Miss Cantrell, presented me with a nametag confirming my status. I was about to slip the tag into my back pocket when she chastised me.

'No, no. You have to actually wear it, displayed in a prominent position. We don't want anyone mistaking you for some creep trying to kidnap one of the kids.'

Even after I had sheepishly pinned the nametag to my shirtfront she gave me that look teachers can't help but give you when you have misbehaved, regardless of your age. I felt like one of the kids from her class who had been caught out doing something wrong. I just didn't know what it was.

She wasn't finished with me. 'I see you don't have a plastic bag with you, for your lunch?' she commented.

A boy ahead of me in the line turned around. He was smiling and seemed joyously happy in the knowledge that it was a parent who was in trouble for a change.

'No. I don't have a plastic bag,' I answered her. 'Should I have one?'

'Your lunch then? Where's your lunch?'

'Well ... I don't have my lunch with me. I was

going to buy something to eat when we get there.'

She was about to chastise me a second time before pursing her lips and saying nothing more, possibly reminding herself that I was actually an independent adult. She chose to roll her eyes sarcastically instead and waved me onto the bus.

The empty seat was alongside a boy who I had seen a few times before, walking home from school on his own. He was the only child who had not joined in the raucous celebrations when the bus took off. He glanced across at me before returning to the book and pencil case nursed on his lap. He unzipped the case, rifled through it, and brought out a red pencil. He went straight to work, colouring in the letters of a name scrawled across the front cover of the book in the design of a graffiti tag — MORGAN.

I watched as he concentrated on his work, skilfully ensuring that he did not draw outside the lines. After he had coloured in the letters of his name he returned the pencil to the case before looking across at me again. 'Who are you?' he asked, rubbing the tip of his nose with the knuckle of a finger.

'I'm Meg's dad. You know Meg?'

We both looked around to where Meg was sitting, just two rows behind us. Not surprisingly she was with her closest friend, Alice. They had been inseparable from their first day of primary school together.

The boy rubbed the end of his nose again, this time with his palm. 'Yeah, I know Meg. And I know you are her father. But what is your name?'

'My name? Oh, I'm Tom.' I pointed to the cover of his book. 'And you're Morgan?'

He picked up the book and hugged it to his chest as he answered me. 'Yeah, Morgan.'

'Is that a colouring book? I said.

He appeared mildly insulted by my suggestion. 'No. Colouring books are for kids. Small kids like my baby sister, Angeline. This is a book of maps.'

'Maps? Can I have a look at them?'

He looked me in the face. As he was assessing my character the bus screeched to a halt. The driver slammed his hand down on the horn and left it there. Morgan and I, and most everyone on the bus, looked out of the window to see what had happened. We had stopped in heavy traffic outside one the city's largest hospitals. The area in front of the hospital's emergency entrance was crowded with cigarette smokers, all huddled around an ashtray about the size of a forty–four gallon drum.

The majority of the smokers were patients wearing blue hospital gowns or pyjamas, or both. Two men in wheelchairs chatted to each other in between puffing furiously at their cigarettes, while one elderly patient, supporting an IV pole slow-dripping glucose into his veins, attempted to roll himself a smoke. He had the cigarette papers balanced in one hand and a tobacco pouch in the other.

As the bus shunted forward, no more than a few feet at a time, Morgan tapped me on the shoulder.

'Do you want to see my maps?'

Without waiting from a response from me he rested the book in his lap and opened it to the first page, to an elaborately designed border that framed a picture of a large garden. A redbrick building had been drawn in the centre of the garden. The building had a bell tower on the top. It looked very similar to our school building. There was also a large tree in the front garden, just like the ghost gum in our schoolyard.

A series of red arrows led away from the school gate. Morgan had drawn several children into the picture. They were walking home from the school. The arrows travelled around the corner, crossed a road and stopped at the front gate of a wooden house. The house had been coloured-in bright green, while the high-pitched roof was nearly as blue as the sky above it. A sign in the front garden of the house announced that it was HOME.

The smiling face of a child looked out of the front window of the house and across the street, to where two children were standing on the footpath holding hands. I pointed to the face in the window. 'Who is this?'

Morgan tapped on the window. 'That's me. I am in the room I share with my older brother, Nelson.'

I looked across the road to where the couple were standing. 'And these two? Who are they?'

Morgan slapped a hand over his mouth as he tried to stop himself from laughing aloud.

'What is it, Morgan? What's funny?' I asked.

He took his hand away from his mouth, cupped his

hands together, leaned across the seat and whispered to me. 'I saw from the window, my brother, Nelson. Here.' He pointed to the couple. 'I saw him kiss his girlfriend here, after school. My mother was away at work. They kissed two times.'

He stuck most of his fist in his mouth as he began laughing again.

When he finally stopped laughing he turned the page to a second drawing. It was another map, and used the same colourful border design. I immediately recognised the picture. It was a detailed study of my own suburb. The major roads had been included, as had the playgrounds, the railway stations, the public library and the swimming pool. A series of arrows criss-crossed the map, linking the playgrounds to each other. The streets were full of people, some walking their dogs, kids kicking a football in a park, and families out strolling together.

A KAPOW! cartoon balloon had been drawn near a swing set at one of the playgrounds. I pointed to it.

'What does this mean, Morgan?'

He hesitated before answering me. 'This is where another boy, a bigger boy than me, he punched me.'

He made a fist and pushed it into his cheek.

'Here. He hit me here.'

I looked back to the map, to the scene of the crime. I could see a boy standing behind a tree in the park. He appeared to be hiding. I pointed to the boy.

'Is this you, Morgan?'

'No. That's the boy who punched me. I have left him in the park until I can come back with my brother.'

The choirgirls along the back seat interrupted our conversation, breaking by into a chant of 'No! no! no! — we want to go — no! no! no!' as the bus was again forced to a halt in the traffic.

Morgan turned the page to the next drawing. It was a map of greater Melbourne and closely resembled a Melway map. Morgan had attached a foldout section to the book. It allowed him to include the suburbs of the outer west and north, across the city to the beach suburbs and distant hills of the east. Another red arrow journey began at Morgan's house and travelled out along the nearby freeway to the airport, which was marked with drawings of several aircraft.

A second journey headed in the opposite direction and wound its way through the city and onto a highway before heading east.

Morgan nodded in the direction of the airport.

'This is where we arrived in Australia. We landed here in the airplane. When I was smaller.'

He followed the second set of arrows from his house. Morgan crossed busy intersections, he travelled over bridges and along empty highways, until he arrived at a spot on the map where a thick black cross had been drawn, marking the end of his destination.

'And this is where my other family live. My cousins and aunties and uncles, they all live here.' He then retraced his steps back to his own house. 'I don't see my cousins anymore. It's a long way to go.'

He quickly turned the page to the next drawing. It was a map of Australia, coloured in various shades of green around the edges and browns and dull yellows across the centre. Each of the states and territories had been mapped and named, as had the capital cities and some natural features, including mountain ranges and rivers. I could see an aircraft flying to the right of ULURU — BIGGEST ROCK IN THE WORLD!

I looked toward the Indian Ocean, located on one edge of the map and coloured a deep green.

'Where are you from, Morgan?'

He answered by turning the page to yet another map, showing the continent of Africa. Each country had been named and shaded in soft colours. Another aeroplane was about to land on a narrow strip of land on the east coast. Morgan touched the aircraft lightly.

'We are from here. My family come from Somalia.'

I could hear a siren approaching us from behind. When an ambulance sped by the bus the children screamed with a mix of excitement and apprehension. The bus driver grabbed a microphone from the dashboard as the bus stopped again.

'Okay kids. Take it easy. We've got a problem up ahead. We'll just have to sit tight for a few minutes.'

Morgan turned the page to the final drawing in the book. It was another large city. The streets were crowded with buses and bicycles and people, and dogs, lots of dogs. I ran a hand over the map.

'There's so much information here, Morgan. You must have a good memory for places?'

He shook his head vigorously.

'No. I don't remember anything about Africa. I was too young when we came. I made this drawing from books with pictures of my country. And stories. Stories from my mother and from my family.'

I followed Morgan's final journey from the airport. It ended abruptly on the far side of the city; at a location also marked with a heavy cross.

'And this is where you lived when you were younger?' I asked him, pointing to the cross.

Morgan said nothing as he slowly closed the book. He picked up a plastic bag from under his seat. It contained his lunch. He put the book in the bag and returned it to the floor. Then he leaned his head against the window and closed his eyes.

When we finally took off again every kid on the bus, from the front seats to the back, broke into spontaneous applause. They quietened almost as quickly when the ambulance sped by a second time with its siren blaring. It was heading in the direction we had just come from.

I realised what had caused our delay when we passed a car wreck in the middle of the next intersection. The roof of the car had been torn open like a can of beans, and the passenger side doors had been crushed in. A tow-truck driver in overalls was sweeping shattered glass from the road, while a fire-fighter hosed down the gutter. A stream of water laced with patterns of dark oil ran towards the drain.

Most of the children moved to one side of the bus and looked out through the window at the accident until Miss Cantrell stood up and loudly clapped her hands together several times.

'Children. Back to your seats.'

Morgan tapped me on the arm. 'The cross in my picture, it's not of my home. We came from our village to the city, so that we could leave for another place.'

He covered the cross with the tip of his finger. 'This is the graveyard.' Morgan looked at me calmly as his chest quietly rose with each breath.

The girls along the back seat broke into another rhythmic clap and chant as soon as they spotted the giant Rubik's Cube out front of the museum.

When the bus pulled into the curb Miss Cantrell got to her feet. 'Okay. Everybody. Now listen. We will get off the bus in pairs. And we will remain in pairs. Hold hands with your partner. And please stay together.'

Meg and Alice stood up. They took each other by the hand, skipped down the aisle, and jumped off the bus. With the exception of the driver, who was waiting in the doorway for everyone to leave, I was the final passenger off the bus. Morgan was waiting for me on the footpath.

# How Sweet the Sound

I didn't expect Benny's sixtieth birthday celebration to be any different from his fifty-ninth. Or his fifty-eighth; or any other birthday, anniversary, or the other usual excuses for a party that my mother organised, three or four times a year, to 'bring the mob together again'. I had long grown tired of the family parties and didn't drink, so I stayed away from most of them, offering up the stock excuse of a cold or flu, or maybe work that couldn't be put off.

But staying away from Benny's sixtieth would not be worth the resulting fallout from my mother, which would go on for weeks. So I had resigned myself to fronting up for the party, even if only for the token effort of an hour or so.

Benny wasn't family, not technically at least. He and my mother got together when they met at a karaoke night ten years earlier at the Chelsea RSL. Benny was out on the town getting pissed with some workmates at the time. It was another birthday celebration, his fiftieth birthday. The story that they often like to tell, over and over again, is that Benny seduced mum with a double vodka and orange and his rendition of Frank Sinatra's 'Witchcraft' — a song that won him first place on the night after a mate bribed the judge with a bottle of Jack Daniels and a tray of T-Bones from the local butcher.

When it came time to announce the winner of the karaoke competition Benny and mum, who had known each other for only a few hours, were arm in arm on the dance floor. When Benny's name was called out over the microphone, the words Las Vegas were unfortunately mentioned among the prizes. My mother had squealed with drunken delight and started jumping up and down, thinking that she had won a stake in a trip to the bright lights of Las Vegas itself.

But it was not to be. First prize was not an overseas trip but an ex-rental copy of an Elvis Presley video, *Live in Las Vegas*. Although briefly disappointed Benny and mum staggered home to her flat in the early hours of the morning, sat on the couch with a beer each, and watched the rhinestoned and flabby Elvis together.

When I called around to see her the next morning, on the way to a netball game with my fourteen-year-old daughter, Stella, Benny was sitting at the kitchen table reading the paper and drinking a can of beer.

'Hair of the dog,' he chuckled with a wink in

Stella's direction as he lifted the can in a mock toast to himself.

There was a second, opened beer sitting on the table in front of the chair across from him. Mum had her back to me as she stood at the kitchen sink, doing the dishes. When she finally turned around to give Stella a kiss on the cheek I noticed that she had a bruise under one eye. I looked over at Benny, who was peering forlornly down into the bottom of his empty can.

When I looked back at my mother's bruised face she gave me the same stare she had presented to me since I was a kid — 'let it be'.

I could stomach no more than a few minutes or so in the flat before excusing myself. 'I've got to get Stella to the game,' I told her.

During the drive to netball Stella rested her head against the passenger-side window and didn't say a word. After we had pulled into the car park alongside the netball courts she looked at me from across the bonnet of the car.

'Dad, did you see Nan's eye?'

'Yeah, I saw it. Come on, grab your bag from the back seat.'

She rested both hands on the bonnet.

'How did it get there?'

'I don't know. Maybe she fell over. You know how she gets when she's been drinking.'

' I bet she didn't fall. Why didn't you ask her?'

I admired my daughter's growing independence and

even her occasional defiance. But her questions about my mother, the company she kept, and her lifestyle made me feel uncomfortable. Stella adored her grandmother and had spent a lot of time being cared for by her when she was younger. But, now that she was growing up, she was beginning to question my mother's destructive behaviour that revolved around drinking and partying most weekends.

'Because she wouldn't want me to ask, Stell. She's never wanted me to ask.'

I began walking away from the car. Stella folded her arms across her chest and refused to move.

'Maybe you should have asked him, that drunk sitting there. I bet he'd know how she got it. I don't like him. You should have told him to leave the flat. I bet he hit her'

I looked down at my watch as I searched for an answer.

'We don't know that. Like I said, she probably fell over or something. Come on, you'll be late for the game. Let's go.'

As I walked around to the passenger side of the car I attempted to drape my arm over Stella's shoulder, as I normally would do, but she backed away from me and walked on ahead.


As I climbed the last flight of stairs to the flat for Benny's birthday party I could hear the old Tom Jones number,

'It's Not Unusual', belting out of the open doorway. It was a bad sign. They generally started with something a little slower, a tune to get the voice box going but not the dancing shoes.

For my mother the opening act of the night had always been Billie Holiday, whose deeply sad voice would sometimes reduce her to tears before the night had even warmed up. For Benny it had to be Hank Williams or Nat King Cole, depending on the crowd and the mood of the party.

Seeing as it was his birthday, Benny got to choose the music, which was a house rule. The party boy or girl always got to pick the music. A belter from Tom Jones indicated that people would already be up on their feet. It also meant that they would have got swinging early, with a few heart-starters at the RSL.

I walked into the flat with a bottle of Polish spirits under my arm. I hadn't bothered gift-wrapping it, so it was still in a bottle-shop brown paper bag. Tess, my wife, couldn't believe that I'd give Benny alcohol for his sixtieth birthday.

'Why grog, Chris? And rocket fuel at that?'

'He's an alcoholic,' I shrugged, as if the reasoning was obvious.

'Exactly! That's what I mean. Why give him more grog?'

'What else would I give him, Tess, a membership for the gym? Anyway, with some luck it will kill him.'

The bottle under my arm was a forty ounce,

ninety percent proof import. While it was capable of battering most people's vital organs to death, I was sure that Benny would survive it. What he didn't finish off tonight he'd probably top up his cornflakes with tomorrow morning.

The usual suspects were all in attendance at the party. Benny's crew from the RSL numbered ten or so no-hopers. They stood out from the crowd, marginally, as they were just a little older than most other guests who had crammed into the flat. They were also a little more bloated around the face. A few of them, those with artificial hips, chronic arthritis or alcohol-induced paralysis, sat in a line along a bench on one side of the room dancing with their hands. They occasionally whacked each other in the face as they waved their arms about erratically.

The furniture in the room had been pushed back against the walls. The dance floor, a worn carpet square in the lounge room, was full, not only with mum and some of Benny's cronies but most of my aunties and uncles and a few cousins and their own kids.

I had arrived on my own as Tess had declined the invitation, preferring to avoid the mayhem by propping at home on the couch and watching telly. The best I could get out of Stella, after begging her to come along with me, was that she agreed to pick me up a few hours later on her way home from dinner with some of her friends from work.

When I handed Benny the bottle of rocket fuel he

ripped it out of the paper bag and licked his lips as he read the label. He held the bottle up to my face.

'You'll have one with me, Christopher?'

I didn't like him calling me Christopher but couldn't be bothered correcting him.

'You know I don't drink, Benny.'

'Come on, come on ... it's my fucking well birthday. The big Six-O. Just this one for ...'

I caught him as he collapsed into my arms. He rested the side of his face against my chest. 'Come on, Chrissie. For Benny Boy. My birthday. Drink up.'

I eased him into a chair and left him mumbling something to himself about a 'big drink', excused myself from the room and joined the line in the hallway waiting for the toilet. Tommy Carr, a mate of Benny's who lived in the flat opposite was in the line in front of me. He looked suspiciously over his shoulder at me. Although I knew Tommy reasonably well he was too drunk to recognise me at all.

He leaned forward and breathed traces of some cheap firewater in my face.

'Who the fuck do you think you're looking at? Are you right? Fucking well right, you cunt?'

Someone tapped me on the shoulder from behind. It was one of my nephews, Harry. He towered over me. He shook my hand, squeezing it tightly. Although it was a cold night, he was wearing only a tight singlet, cut-down jean shorts, and a pair of thongs. He was also well muscled. Harry had the build of a middleweight.

'You been working out or something, Harry? On the weights?' I asked, looking him up and down.

He flexed his biceps with pride. Then I noticed that he had a young girl with him. He had his arm over her shoulder in a loose headlock. He pushed her toward me.

'This is my girl, Angie. Angie, meet my uncle Chris. My old man's brother.'

He tightened the headlock a little, forcing the girl's head downward.

'I call her Angel though. She's my sweet angel, aren't you, babe?'

With that Harry planted a kiss on the back of her head.

Tommy Carr had finished in the toilet. He came out with, not only his fly open, but the front of his pants unbuttoned as well. As he passed by me he hitched his pants up around his waist and glared at me again.

'You fucking right, I said? Are you?'

I was about to go into the toilet when Harry tapped me on the shoulder again.

'Hey Chris? Can Angel get in there ahead of you? Don't want to push in but she's busting for a piss.'

As I motioned Angel by me with the sweep of an arm I noticed two things about her. Firstly, she was very young. Maybe about thirteen or fourteen but no older. And she was built like a wafer. Harry was nineteen, almost twenty. He was also a big nineteen. And he was already old. As Angel was about to close the door I got a clearer look at her face under the harsh light of the toilet's bare bulb. She had a large bruise sitting in the centre of one cheek, in the shape of a fist.

After she had closed the door behind her I turned to Harry.

'Your girlfriend? Angie? Sorry, Angel, is it? What happened to her face, Harry?'

Harry gave me that look you get from someone mentally scratching their brain for an answer that might cover their arse. He gave up scratching, preferring to say nothing, so I persevered.

'The girl's face? What happened to her face, Harry? It's all bruised.'

He smiled at me and raised his eyes.

'Oh that. She fell over. She works in a supermarket. She slipped over on some mess or something. She's real clumsy sometimes, the Angel.'

Harry was aware that I didn't believe a word he'd said. He didn't care, though. He had offered me an excuse. That was all he needed to do and he knew it. He looked away from me as the toilet door opened. He took Angel by the hand and walked back into the lounge without another word to me.

I'd had more than enough of the party. I called Stella on my mobile to let her know I was ready to be picked up. She didn't answer, so I left a message for her. When she still hadn't turned up fifteen minutes later I decided to walk down to the highway and hail a cab.

I hadn't spoken a word to my mother since arriving, as she was too busy enjoying herself to notice my presence. I managed to catch her attention between yet another Tom Jones number and the introduction of Tina Turner. They were upping the stakes.

'Mum. I'm off home. Tess has been sick all week. I'd best get back to her.'

She glared at me. She knew I was bullshitting.

'Sick? She's always sick, that wife of yours. You should have her put down. For her own good.'

She noticed my obvious discomfort and slapped me on the arm.

'Only joking, Chris.' She peered around the door into the kitchen. 'But you can't go yet, son. This is for Benny, his sixtieth.'

'Sorry Mum, but I have to.'

I'd left my exit just a fraction too late. As my mother grabbed me by the arm and urged me to stay a little longer, one of my aunties carried a birthday cake from the kitchen into the lounge. It had a single lit candle on the top. When he saw the cake, Tommy Carr jumped up on one of the lounge chairs and announced that it was time for all of us to sing 'Happy Birthday'.

'You can't leave now. Not now,' my mother winked at me. 'There'll be a slice of cake for you after this is done. You've always loved your cake, son.'

After several renditions of 'Happy Birthday' we were forced to put up with another party tradition; Benny insisted on singing a song of his own as a response to the generosity afforded him, which, that night was a stumbling version of 'Mona Lisa'.

Benny was no Nat King Cole but it didn't curb him. He howled the song like a dog with a broken paw but no one seemed to mind. Several of the guests actually shed a few tears, including Benny himself. And when he'd finished singing, those who did not applaud repeated the words, 'Beautiful, Benny, beautiful,' over and over to themselves.

As I was about to finally escape the flat, Harry stepped forward into the centre of the room. He put two fingers in his mouth and let out a piercing whistle.

'Everyone. Everyone. My girlfriend, Angel.'

The girl had been standing timidly behind Harry. He gripped her by a slender arm and dragged her into the centre of the room, and then waited for the crowd to quieten.

'My girlfriend here, Angel, she wants to sing a song for Pop Benny's birthday.' He pushed her lightly in the back as a means of encouragement. 'Go on, Angel, sing.'

The room gradually hushed as Angel dropped her arms to her side. She then took a deep breath and nervously rolled up the sleeves of the hooded windcheater she was wearing. She stood directly under the lounge room light. I could see that not only was her face deeply bruised, it was also badly swollen. She took another breath as people in the room began calling out to her.

'Come on, girl, give us a song.'

It took only the first few notes of the hymn 'Amazing Grace' for everyone to realise that Angel had an exceptional singing voice. As she went on, demands of 'shhh … shhh' went around the room.

She sang quite softly but her voice had no trouble lifting above the crowd. As the melody filled the room, the damage she had suffered became more obvious to me. I could see that she also had faded marks of a previous beating under both eyes, while her lower arms were covered with series of fine horizontal cuts extending from just below her elbows to her wrists. I looked around the room to see who else had noticed the bruises and cuts. They appeared to have seen nothing. Those who were not smiling widely at her had their eyes closed as they swayed gently from side to side.

When Angel had finished her song there was a moment of silence in the room followed by an outbreak of applause and whistling. Harry proudly stepped forward and put his arms around her. I turned to look at my mother. She winked at me again.

'He's done well, young Harry has. She's a little ripper that one. Be family one day. If we're lucky.'

She then looked over to the door leading out into the passageway. 'You'd best be off, Chrissy. Here's your Stella. Why's she being a snob, standing all the way over there? Tell her to get over here and give her Nan a kiss. Then she can get you home before you turn back into that miserable old pumpkin.'

Mum walked away from me and called out across the room, 'Where's my drink, Benny Boy, where's my drink?'

People began calling out 'More! More!' With a few

words of encouragement from Harry, Angel took a few deep breaths before beginning another song, 'Nothing Compares To U.'

Stella was standing in the doorway listening to the girl sing. She called across the room to me.

'Come on, Dad, I'm double parked.'

My mother had circled the room and was back with a fresh glass of beer. She grabbed Stella by the arm and kissed her on the cheek just as the girl suddenly stopped singing. Harry prodded her to go on.

'Come on, sing for them, Angel.'

The girl slumped her head forward and dropped her hands to her sides.

'I can't. I've forgotten the words.'

Harry looked around the room with embarrassment as the crowd urged the girl to go on. She shook her head from side to side and mouthed the word 'no' to Harry. He grabbed her by the arm and jerked her toward him as he whispered something in her ear. Then he took her roughly by the hand and pulled her through the crowd. They walked behind Stella and left the flat.

I repeated my excuse to my mother about Tess being sick, avoided Benny completely, and left the party with no goodbyes to my relatives. We walked downstairs towards Stella's car. Harry was standing alone at the bottom of the dimly lit stairwell, smoking a cigarette. He looked up at me and said, 'See you, uncle Chris,' while glancing menacingly at Stella without appearing to recognise her. She ignored him completely.

It was raining outside. As we drove out of the street the car's headlights picked up the outline of someone sitting at a bus shelter on the service road alongside the on-ramp to the highway. Stella looked out through the front windscreen.

'There's that girl, Dad, the singer from the party. Do you think we should stop?'

While I hesitated Stella eased her car into the kerb. She got out and walked over to the girl. They spoke for a few minutes. I watched through the glass as Stella rifled through her bag and handed the girl a tissue before taking her phone from her bag. She made a call and then came back to the car. She gestured to me to wind down the window.

'We'll have to give her a lift. I tried calling her a cab. There's no answer. They're probably busy because of all the rain. She says she wants to go home.'

'Where's that?' I asked.

'Somewhere in the city, she says. Some shelter. And she needs some money, Dad. She's got nothing.'

'I don't know if we should …'

'We're not going to leave her here, Dad. Come on, give me the money.'

I looked over at the bus shelter before taking a twenty-dollar note from my wallet and passing it though the window. Stella opened the back door of the car before walking back to the shelter. She sat down next to the girl and handed her the money. They got up. The girl jumped in the back seat and slid across to the other side of the car and rested her head against the side window.

She didn't say a word during the drive into the city. We dropped her near Flinders Street station. As she was about to get out of the car Stella turned around and grabbed the girl by the arm.

'Will you be all right here? It's pretty late.'

The girl peered out into the street, but still didn't say a word. The late night noise of the street was buzzing all around us. The girl jumped from the car and ran along the footpath. We watched her until she became lost somewhere in the crowd.

As we drove home Stella began questioning me.

'Who was she with, that girl?'

'You saw her. She was with Harry, your cousin.'

'She's his girlfriend?'

'I suppose so. Looked liked it. They were with each other. Yeah.'

'She has a lovely singing voice, that girl.'

'Yeah, she has a wonderful voice,' I answered, knowing where the interrogation was heading.

I felt relieved that Stella said nothing more on our drive home. But when we turned the corner into our street she asked another question.

'Her face? Did you see her face, Dad?'

'Her face?'

Stella rolled her eyes in frustration.

'Her face was all blue and swollen on one side. You must have seen it? And those arms? She's cutting herself.

You saw those marks.'

'Yeah, I saw them.'

'Well, what do you think?' she demanded. 'Why would she be cutting herself like that?'

I turned away from and looked out through the windscreen.

'I don't know, love. I don't even know the girl.'

Stella pulled into the driveway, turned off the car and slumped into her seat. I opened the door and was about to get out when she tapped me on the shoulder. I turned around expecting another question but she just looked at me as if she was waiting for me to say something. When I didn't, she jumped out of the car and slammed the door, leaving me alone in the darkness. I was about to get out of the car when I noticed something on the back seat. I leaned across and picked it up. It was a bloodied tissue.

Once I was inside the house I threw the tissue in the bin under the kitchen sink and washed my hands clean in warm water and soap. Tess was sitting up in bed reading a book. She lowered her head and looked at me over the top of her glasses.

'How was the party?'

'Don't ask.'

'That good? Sorry I missed it.'

I got into bed and buried my head in the pillow.

# The Chocolate Empire

The summer was hot and dry. When my best friend
Connie and I weren't at Richmond pool we hung out
at the river. With nobody around to keep an eye on
us and no rules to follow, we felt free. Freedom meant
taking risks, like jumping from every bridge across the
Yarra, from Princes Bridge in the city to Kane's swing
bridge at Studley Park.

What the river didn't have was girls. They stayed
away from the mud and the water rats, the rubbish and
the weeds. And seeing as the girls wouldn't come to us,
we occasionally drifted back to the pool looking for
them.

I was sitting with my back to a low brick wall
dividing the sundeck from the swimming pool, alongside
Connie. He studied his biceps as Jeanie Rizzo walked
by, hand-in-hand with Rita Cole. They were wearing

cutdown Levis, bikini tops and bare feet — the uniform of the summer. The girls stopped across the deck from us and sat down. Jeanie lit a cigarette while Rita threw her towel out across the concrete sundeck.

I couldn't take my eyes off Jeanie as she dragged on the cigarette and blew smoke into the air. She looked just like a model in a cigarette ad. Her skin was wet and tanned and straps of long dark hair were plastered across her breasts.

Jeanie handed Rita the packet of cigarettes. She lit up and held the cigarette in one hand as she picked specks of gravel from her thighs with the other. I could see that the JM scar on her arm had not faded. She had burnt it into her skin with the end of a Redhead match earlier in the year on hearing that Jim Morrison had died. The sudden death of the lead singer of The Doors sent most girls from our school into a dark mourning.

I tapped Connie on the shoulder and nodded across the sundeck.

'Hey Connie? See Rita over there. You ever thought of asking her out? We could double date. You and Rita and Jeanie and me at the movies.'

Connie looked up just as Jeanie flipped from her back onto her stomach. As she lay down on her towel she cupped a breast in each hand and lifted them forward.

'The movies? And how would we get there, Joe, on the back of your bike? They wouldn't come near us unless we had a car and enough money to shout both of them all night. Stop dreaming, Joe. We've got no hope.'

'Got nothing to do with a car, Connie. You're just too scared.'

Before he could reply, Jeanie and Rita jumped up and headed back to the pool.

We didn't see them again until the Saturday after New Year. Connie and me were standing out front of the hamburger joint on Church Street where his father played cards. Waiting with Connie for his old man to come out of the club was sometimes an all day affair. He didn't like to leave the card table when he was on a winning streak and refused to leave it if he was losing — until he either got back in front or lost the lot.

I looked along the street when I heard Buster Morrison's metallic blue FB roar by the club. Its fat chromed hubs shimmered against the dark bitumen. Buster drove for a crew of older teenagers who hung out at the Venus espresso bar on Bridge Road. They had all left school, had jobs and money, and spent their time cruising the streets for girls.

My heart sunk when I spotted Jeanie in the back seat of Buster's car wedged between two boys. Connie muttered, 'Fuck me' when he saw Rita Cole riding up front with her arm draped over Buster's shoulder. The car ran a red light at the Bridge Road intersection and gunned up the Church Street hill. We watched as it vanished over the ridge of the hill.

'See,' Connie screamed as he threw his hands in the air.

'You want a girl, you got to get hold of a car.'

'A car? What would we do with a car, Connie? When it came time to drop the girls home you could steer while they got out and helped me push'

'Don't be a smart arse, Joe. It's not my fault I can't drive. Anyway, *you* can't drive, either.'

'Right. Me either. So, let me tell you what we could do. We can borrow my old man's car and sit in it all night, out the front of my place. It's a Hillman, Connie, a fucking Hillman. We could sit there with Jeanie and Rita and listen to the radio. That way my mum won't have to look far when it gets late.'

I waited out on the street while Connie went into the club to collect some money from his father. When he back came out he walked to the edge of the footpath and looked along the strip of road where the FB had driven by. He kicked an empty beer can along the gutter and swore a little more. He was about to take another swipe at the can when his dad came out of the club and yelled at him.

'Con. Don't do that. Look at the time. Get home, will ya, or I'll kick your arse. Your mother's waiting for the shopping money.'

He gave me a dirty look. Connie's dad didn't like us hanging around together. Neither did my father. It wasn't that he had anything against Connie in particular, not that I knew of, at least. He didn't discriminate against any of my friends. He didn't like any of them.

When the new school year came around we weren't ready for it. Rita Cole didn't turn up for the first day of school and by lunchtime a story had gone around the schoolyard that she had got herself pregnant over the holidays and that her family had shipped her off to some relation in the country. Jeanie Rizzo was at school but she didn't so much as glance at any of us boys, let alone say a word. She was suddenly years ahead of the rest of us.

Connie said that you could tell by the way she walked that Jeanie was, 'Doing it … day and night, I'd bet. You watch those hips sway from side to side, Joe. A dead giveaway.'

She soon followed Rita's lead and had left the school by the middle of the year. I occasionally saw her around the suburb over the following year. And then one day she was gone for good.

The school was just a few years old and had been built on an old tip site alongside the river. It occupied a narrow strip of land between a road bridge at one end of the school and a rail bridge at the other. The school had been erected on land-fill. Forty-feet deep foundations had been driven into the earth before the three-storey building went up. It would remain safe unless the foundations of the building were inundated by the waters of a catastrophic flood. 'A flood of Biblical proportions,' our Geography teacher, Mr Simmonds, liked to quote each time he talked about the ancient landscapes of the river and its surrounds.

On rainy winter days we would look down at the river from the vantage point of our classroom and pray that the waters would rise up and sweep the building away — after we had been evacuated or gone home for the day, of course.

At recess and at lunchtime, a group of us — the smokers — would slip through a hole in the wire fence behind the gym and follow a dirt track, overgrown with wild fennel, along the river. We'd meet in the shadows of a bluestone arch that supported the rail bridge over the river. The bridge was known locally as the Catwalk, in honour of the many strays that used it to move between the poorer side of the river — our side — and the eastern suburbs of Melbourne. Those cats were smart. They understood that the rubbish bins of leafy Hawthorn provided richer pickings than a whole tip full of garbage could offer, on our side of the river.

The river was technically off-limits but Connie, me and another kid, Henry Harrison, couldn't stay away from it. Henry loved telling stories and seemed to know more tales about the river than Mark Twain. He lived in a house on the high side of the river that the rest of us from school never got to visit. He had been at our school for only a year, after being expelled from the private school he'd been at, when he was caught breaking into the science lab. He'd set the mice free that were to be cut into hundreds of pieces the next day.

'It was going to be a mass execution,' he explained to me when he told me the story on the day we met while standing in line, waiting to go into class. I was pretty sure that he'd made the story up but I didn't mind. It was a good story.

'Are you an animal lover or something?' I'd asked him.

'No. I just hated my science teacher.'

'Why?'

'I'm not sure, but he looked just like my dad. Maybe that was it?'

During the first weeks back at school the river teased us with its rich scent, drifting into classrooms on the northerly breeze. At lunchtimes and as soon as the last bell of the day had rung out across the schoolyard we headed for the bluestone ledge beneath the Catwalk for a swim and a smoke. With summer almost over we were desperate to take what was left of it, so the short swims soon turned into whole days of wagging for Connie, Henry, and me.

We even considered giving up school altogether. Connie was all for it but not Henry. After a long discussion one night under the bridge we realised that we had little choice but to return to school. Not because we were particularly conscientious but because none of us were willing to face the alternative. School dropouts from our suburb ended up with either a dirty factory job, or casual work hosing down sheep shit at the abattoir yards.

Connie came up with the idea that we would only go back to school after one last day of freedom, which would begin with a swim in the river, followed by a jump from the steel railing of the Catwalk into the water fifty feet below. We met in the park across from the school early the next morning. The sky was clear and the sun was already warm. All too aware that it would be the last swim of the summer, we took as much time as we could walking the dirt track between the railway line and the wild blackberry bushes along the edge of the park.

When I reached the river's edge I looked upstream and watched the gentle current heading our way. I looked up to the rail bridge above me and took several deep breaths as I was reminded of a terrible thought that I often had; that one day this would all be over, and not only for the summer.

We stripped down to our underpants and jumped into the water. I swam to the middle of the river, rolled onto my back and floated with the lazy current. I looked up at the sun and watched as it rose into the sky. Knowing that by the time it was above us it would be almost time for us to leave the river I willed it to stay where it was for a little longer. After a long swim we took up position along the bluestone ledge under the bridge, dangling our feet in the water as we shared a cigarette and listened to a train rumbling overhead as it crossed the bridge.

Each time a train crossed the bridge a flock of pigeons rose up from the web of steel framing that supported the bridge and flew in a wide arc along the river valley before turning for home. I had often wondered why the birds never seemed to get used to the noise of the trains, seeing as they rattled across the bridge over and over again, every day and night of the week. I followed the flight of the birds until they had returned to their roost directly above us.

I took a greedy drag on the cigarette, passed it to Connie and laid back on the warm bluestone. Connie took a drag himself and flicked the cigarette butt into the water. He stood up and unhitched the end of the Tarzan rope from the rusted metal spike that some boy must have driven into the bluestone column of the bridge many years ago. As he left the ledge and swung out on the rope above the water Connie let out a wild 'whoop' before letting go of the rope and crashing into the water. Henry followed Connie off the rope and then I followed him. For the next hour or so we repeatedly scaled the bank from the water back to the rope, swung out over the river, and crashed into the water.

We exhausted ourselves.

With the sun directly above us we left our clothes in a pile on the ledge, climbed back onto the track, then onto the railway line and walked to the centre of the bridge. I looked down at the water. It was a long way. I could see the reflection of the trees beside the riverbank in the water along with the ball of sun.

Connie nudged me in the ribs.

'You ready to jump, Joe?'

'Yep.'

He turned to Henry, who we both knew had never

had the courage to jump from this height before.

'What about you, Henry. You ready? You can walk back if you like and go home and read a book.'

Henry looked down at the water and then defiantly over at Connie.

'Fuck you. I'm ready.'

I slapped my fists against my chest.

'Okay. Let's go. You go left, Henry. Connie, to the right. I don't want one of you landing on me and knocking me out. On the count of three.'

Before I could start the count Henry interrupted. He pointed to the school

'See that? What is it?'

'Stop stalling for time,' Connie teased him. 'You jumping or not?'

'I'm not stalling, arsehole. Take a look.'

A dark band filled the bottom of the sky in the distance.

'What's that, do you reckon?' Henry asked again. 'Rain?'

I didn't know what it was. I just hoped that it was not going to rain on my river today.

'It's probably smoke,' I answered. 'Might be a warehouse fire down around Collingwood? Remember that big fire at the old Skipping Girl factory last winter? The smoke covered half the city.'

'It's not a fire,' Henry answered. 'The smoke's the wrong colour, not dark enough.'

'Jesus fucking Christ. Now you're a scientist,'

Connie sneered. 'I don't care if it's rain or smoke. Let's jump before the next train comes.'

So we took our final leap for the summer. Henry hooted with joy and fear all the way down before hitting the water with a mighty splash. We swam to the riverbank and dressed slowly, looking down occasionally at the tea-stained water. When we had put our clothes back on, we turned our backs on the river and walked away.

Henry, who was trailing behind us called out, 'So, what are we going to do now? Want to go over to Herring Island?'

'We just got dressed,' Connie turned and yelled back at him. 'Anyway, there's nothing over there.'

'There is something over there,' Henry fired back. 'What about the hidden money?'

'Not the buried treasure story again,' groaned Connie. 'Everyone knows that story's bullshit, Henry.'

Herring Island was in the middle of the river, a few bends along from the Catwalk. The island belonged to the water authority but it had not been used for many years. A couple of rusting tinnies were left moored at the island's small jetty and a few sheds and a workshop remained on the island. It had been taken over by a group of homeless men who sheltered in the sheds. They were sometimes seen rowing to and from the island in one of the boats with supplies of food and beer, and in wintertime smoke from their fire drifted across the water.

A story had been going around for years that one of the homeless men had been a rich businessman who lived in a Toorak mansion, until the day he went mad, drew his money out of the bank, put it in a couple of suitcases and buried it on the island. According to the story he lives there now with other derros, including a couple of metho drinkers.

Henry wouldn't let the story rest.

'How do you know the story's bullshit, Connie? I asked my father and even he's heard about it. He says the man was a multi-millionaire who used to run a chocolate empire. And then he vanished into thin air. Hasn't been seen since.'

'A chocolate empire?' Connie laughed. 'None of those derros over on the island ever been millionaires. They're all drunks and no-hopers.'

I wasn't interested in any hidden treasure story but venturing over to the island would mean another swim in the river, so I was all for it.

'Come on, Connie. Why don't we go over there and take a look around. We can ditch our clothes in the old drain across from the abattoir and then swim over.'

When I said those words, 'We could swim over there,' Connie's eyes lit up. He shrugged his shoulders.

'Okay. We'll swim over. But if we find more than a few scraps of tin I'll kiss Henry's arse.'

Henry slapped the back of his school pants.

'Well pucker up then, boy. I'm going to make us rich.'

We walked along the road that followed the course of the river, ducking into bushes on the side of the road each time that a car approached, just in case it was a snooping teacher on the lookout for waggers.

By the time we reached the bank across from the island the sun had disappeared. It now looked like it was certain to rain but I didn't say a word about it, as I was sure it would be a curse on our adventure. We stripped down to our underwear again, shoved our school uniforms into the dry, brick-walled drain, and began swimming across to the island.

Henry wasn't a strong swimmer. While I sometimes suspected that Connie would have left him for dead, I swam alongside Henry whenever we crossed the river. I didn't particularly feel like a hero but I didn't want to have to explain a drowned schoolmate to the police or my parents. Especially when I wasn't supposed to be on the river myself.

Henry tired before we reached the island. He flipped onto his back, sucked at the air and desperately kicked at the water.

'You okay?' I asked, as I treaded water next to him.

'Course I am,' he screamed at me, obviously embarrassed.

When we finally reached the wooden jetty, I helped Henry climb the ladder out of the water. He sat down on the jetty and tried catching his breath. The sky was so dark that when I looked down river, towards the city, its skyscrapers were lit up as bright as night. Connie looked into the sky.

'What's going on, you think?'

A clap of thunder followed by a streak of lighting slicing the sky answered him.

We had only begun to explore the island when the downpour started. It had been so long since we had seen rain that we threw our heads back, screamed into the dark sky, and stomped around in the quickly formed puddles.

The rain was so heavy that I could no longer see across to the far bank where we had hidden our clothes. The wind had also shifted, to the south, and was biting at my skin. I pointed to one of the old sheds.

'Fuck this. Let's shelter in there until it stops.'

We ran across a yard to the shed. I threw the door open and ran inside. Henry, who was last into the shed, slammed the door behind him and joined Connie and me. Connie was pointing a finger. I jumped back when I spotted the old man seated at a table in the corner reading a newspaper. He turned his head slightly in our direction, waited, and then returned to his newspaper, as if we weren't there at all. I took a look around the shed. It was furnished with old armchairs, a floral couch, a small stove and even an old cast-iron bed in one corner. The walls were covered in sports pictures and newspaper headlines.

The old man calmly took off his glasses and looked across the room at three teenage boys covered in mud and freezing to death, wearing nothing but our underwear. He said something but I couldn't hear a word as the noise of the rain beating down on the tin roof was deafening. Then he stood up and walked towards us. Henry, who was standing next to me, grabbed hold of my arm and began to shake uncontrollably, from both cold and fear.

'Are you the chocolate King?' Henry blurted out nervously, as the old man stopped in front of him, leaning forward and poking a finger in his direction.

The old man put a hand behind one ear as he strained to hear what Henry had said.

'The what?'

'Are you the man with the chocolate empire?' Henry shouted. 'The millionaire, with all the money buried …'

His voice fell away as the old man tilted his head to the side and gave Henry a queer look.

'A millionaire?' He looked around the shed and laughed out loud. 'Do you reckon I'd be living here if I was a millionaire? Only if I was as mad crazy as a dog with distemper. You thick in the head or something, kid?'

'Maybe,' Henry mumbled.

The old man turned to Connie and me and looked us up and down.

'Well, I suppose you lot are escapees. Where'd you break out from?'

Connie seemed delighted to be mistaken for an

escaped convict.

'School. We escaped from high school.'

'Good move, good move,' the old man winked at him. 'You're safe here. Quite safe here.'

Henry suddenly screamed and pointed to the ground.

'Look at that, Joe. Jesus, look at that.'

I looked down. Water was streaming under the door and into the shed.

'Shit,' the old man cried, as he rushed by us and opened the door. It looked as if most of the island had disappeared. All I could see were some old metal drums floating by the shed and some trees in the distance.

'Where's the island?' Henry cried. 'Where's it gone?'

'Come on,' the old man called back to us, 'help me with the boat.'

We followed him around to the back of the shed, to where a near rusted-out tinnie was standing on its end, roped to an old gum tree. He unhitched the boat, laid it down, and placed a single wooden oar in the bottom.

'Come on. We'll push her until she floats. Then we'll all jump in. Best make for that far bank before the rain washes down from upstream. There's gonna be no island soon enough.'

He went to the back of the boat and was about to push it forward when he stood up.

'Hang on, I've got to grab some supplies. One of you take hold of this rope so we don't lose her.'

He handed me the rope and went back into the shed. As soon as he was gone Connie screamed.

'I'm not getting in that boat. Look at it, Joe. It'll sink on us.'

'Me either,' Henry added. 'He's pissed, that old bloke. I can smell it on him.'

When the old man came back out of the shed he had a bottle of beer and an opener in one hand and a pouch of tobacco in the other. He slipped the bottle opener and tobacco inside his jacket and popped the bottle of beer in one of the side pockets of the jacket.

'Come on, boys, we're off.'

'We're not going,' Connie said. 'This boat's not seaworthy.'

The old man shrugged his shoulders dismissively as he looked around at what was left of the rapidly disappearing island.

'Well, son, we're not going to sea. We're only heading out on the river. But suit yourselves, boys. Stay as long as you like, but I'm off.'

With that he took the rope from me and began walking the boat to deeper water.

'Wait,' I yelled. 'We're coming.'

With the current stronger than I had ever seen it, the old man used the oar to steer us down river in the direction of the city. For a moment I imagined that small boat, with us in it, being crushed by a tanker in the middle of the bay. But the old man knew what he was doing. As he manoeuvred the oar through the water the boat was gradually carried across river until it hit the far bank at a bend downstream from where we had gone into the water.

The three of us ran back along the riverbank, leaving the old man to tie his boat up at a tree. We reached the drain where we had hidden our clothes only to find a torrent of water raging from its mouth, spewing the rubbish of the street into the river; tin cans, beer bottles, cigarette butts and cardboard boxes.

I had no idea what we should do. I looked back to the old man and his boat. He had taken the opener out of his jacket. He ripped the top off the beer bottle and took a long drink from it. The rain had stopped and the late afternoon sun had punched a hole in the clouds. It was shining on the old man.

The water continued to rise, forcing us to move onto the roadway as the riverbank gradually disappeared.

'Where do you reckon our school uniforms might be?' Connie wondered, as he wrapped his arms around his body, shivering with cold and looking downstream. 'And my shoes? My mum will kill me when I get home.'

The three of us searched the river for items of clothing. In addition to the rubbish washed down from the street, the river was littered with broken tree branches, planks of wood, some old car tyres and a yellow plastic rubbish bin. But no school uniforms or shoes.

I glanced across at Henry. He looked ridiculous. His lips had turned blue with the cold air, he had mud and scratches all over his body, and several twigs and even a bird feather were stuck in his hair.

'Well, we're fucked now, aren't we, Joe? We're fucked.'

I looked across to the island. There was little left to see above the waterline except the tops of the larger trees and the shed roofs.

# Two Men and Their Dogs

Slavoj squeezed himself into the metal seat of the swing-set in the centre of the playground. He searched the pockets of his jacket for his cigarettes and lighter as the dog sniffed around at his feet. Slavoj lit up and watched as the dog cocked its leg against the rusting frame of the play equipment and squirted a stream of steaming piss against the cold steel of the frostbitten morning.

Pleased with its effort in marking its territory, the dog dug its back feet into the ground and kicked and scratched around in the dirt before rolling onto its back in an attempt to seduce Slavoj into leaning forward from his seat and tickling its stomach.

He had been told that the dog was an Australian terrier of sorts, although the origin of the various 'sorts' was apparently unknown. It was black and tan in colour except for the occasional fleck of dull grey, which gave it an aged and slightly forlorn appearance. But the dog wasn't old. It just looked that way.

Slavoj had involuntarily inherited the dog from the old woman who had lived in the flat across the landing. She went into hospital after falling on the stairs. The woman had been taken away in an ambulance and never returned to the estate. He had listened to the cries of the dog coming from inside the flat for two days, before accepting that he had to do something to rescue it. Reluctantly, Slavoj reported the cries of the dog to one of the cleaners, who did little more than dismiss him.

'I can't understand a word you're fucking saying, mate. You got a complaint? Not my business, mate. Ring Client Services. Number's on the board there, in the foyer where the lifts are. You got a complaint, ring them. Tell them your troubles, not me. I'm just here to mop the floors and get rid of the rubbish.'

But Slavoj didn't want to complain to anyone. He wasn't sure what 'Client Services' referred to but he did have the sense to know that he didn't want to bring himself to their attention.

After speaking to the cleaner Slavoj avoided the lift and walked the five flights of stairs to his flat. He could hear the frantic barking of the dog before he reached his landing. He fumbled with his keys as he opened the door to his flat. When the dog heard the key in the lock it began to cry even more frantically. Slavoj took his jacket off and turned to shut the door. He hesitated before accepting what it was he had to do.

He looked along the windswept landing before trying the old woman's front door. It was locked. The dog sniffed and scratched at the bottom of the door in its attempt to get to him. Slavoj lifted a hand to the side of his face and looked into the flat through the kitchen window. Immediately the dog jumped from the floor onto the kitchen sink and knocked against the glass with its front paws. Slavoj pressed both palms against the glass. The window was stiff but it wasn't locked.

He hadn't lifted the window more than a few inches before the dog threw itself onto its side and began to squeeze its way under the frame.

As soon as he got it back to his flat, Slavoj grabbed a bowl from the drying rack on the sink and filled it with water. The dog had drunk most of the water from the bowl before it started coughing and spluttering. Slavoj refilled the bowl and returned it to the floor. The dog took a slower drink this time, lapping at the bowl with its tongue. It sniffed around the boundary of the kitchen, lifted its head and trotted into the only other room of the bed-sitter. The dog mapped the room with the point of its nose before stopping in the middle of the room, raising its leg and pissing on the leg of the coffee table.

'Ach!' Slavoj slammed his foot on the floor and clapped his hands together.

The dog ran under the couch. It crawled along on its stomach until it was wedged between the back of the couch and the wall. Slavoj got down on his hands and knees. He could see the dog's yellow, terrified eyes staring back at him from the darkness.

He went into the kitchen and rifled through the cupboards for something to feed it. He settled on a mix of broken bread, warm milk and beaten raw egg. He put the bowl on the floor in the kitchen and went back into the other room to get the dog. It hadn't moved from its secure hiding place.

Slavoj brought the bowl of food into the room and placed it on the floor in front of the couch. He sat in a chair on the opposite side of the room and lit a cigarette. He had smoked a second cigarette and still there was no movement from beneath the couch. He got down on his hands and knees, rested the side of his face on the floor and looked into the eyes of the dog.

He began patting the cold tiles of the floor with an open hand in an effort to entice it to come out and eat. It did not move. Slavoj whistled — a long, low whistle that he remembered from when he was a young boy. It was a similar whistle to the one his father had used to call the cows in of a night.

Slavoj whistled a second time. He saw the dog's ears lift like a shadow puppet. It began to crawl slowly forward on its stomach towards the bowl of food until the front half of its body protruded from under the couch. It lifted its nose and cautiously sniffed the air before crawling across to the bowl. Then it got to its feet, sniffed at the food, and stopped. The dog looked directly at Slavoj, tilting its head to one side as it did. Slavoj gestured toward the bowl with his hand. The dog moved away from the bowl, looked again at Slavoj, and then moved cautiously forward again before burying its head in the bowl.

It didn't stop eating until the bowl had been licked clean. When it finally looked up at Slavoj it was wearing a milky egg and milk beard.

That night Slavoj put a cardboard box on the floor in the kitchen and lined it with newspaper. But as he always slept with the bedroom door open, Slavoj woke in the night to the weight of the dog resting its head against his thigh.

The unused box remained on the floor under the kitchen table.


Slavoj finished his cigarette and stood up from the kid's swing-seat. He buried his hands in his coat pockets, whistled to the dog, and began walking toward the entrance to his block. He was about to walk through the door and into the foyer when he noticed that the dog had not followed him as it usually did. He walked back towards the playground.

It surprised Slavoj to see the terrier trotting around in circles. It was trailing a larger dog that also came to the playground most mornings during the week. The first time he saw the larger dog enter the playground from a narrow side street, Slavoj thought that this squat, fat animal was a wild pig, similar to those from the forests of his homeland.

It wasn't a pig but a dark, brindle-coated, heavy-set animal unlike any dog Slavoj had seen before. Its owner, an elderly white-bearded man, who hid his face under a beaten woollen cap and turned-up collar, accompanied the dog to the playground each morning.

The two dogs had managed to avoid each other until this morning, as the small terrier, somewhat like Slavoj, mostly kept to itself.

Slavoj watched as the two dogs circled each other with increasing excitement. They were barking at each other, not out of fear or threat, but joy. Slavoj shook his head and wondered why the small terrier had suddenly decided to befriend the larger dog. The other dog's owner was sitting on a bench, laughing to himself as he watched the dogs entangle themselves in each other's legs before jumping up and running around and around in circles again.

As the two dogs played Slavoj could overhear two men talking behind him. He looked over his shoulder. It was the cleaner from the flats, talking to another man wearing a suit and tie. The man in the suit was also talking on his mobile phone. The cleaner pointed out through the doorway, in the direction of Slavoj, who looked back towards the dogs. They were lying on their sides, facing each other. The big dog was licking the terrier's face.

Slavoj walked toward the dogs, whistling to the terrier as he did. It wouldn't stop playing, so he began calling it in between the increasingly desperate whistles.

'Dog. Dog. Come.'

The old man on the bench looked up at Slavoj and then past him, in the direction of the foyer. Slavoj looked over his shoulder. The man in the suit was walking across the grass towards them. The cleaner stood watching from the doorway, leaning on a broom.

Slavoj clapped his hands together and shouted.

'Dog! Come! Come!'

The old man stood up from the bench and slowly raised his hand towards Slavoj.

'It's okay. They're only having a play. Let 'em go. They're just having a play.'

Slavoj couldn't understand much of what the old man was saying. He was concentrating on the man bearing down on him. He was certain that he must have come for him, for Slavoj. He was about to reach down for the terrier when he heard a voice behind him.

'The dog? Is that your dog, sir?'

Slavoj turned around. The man in the suit pointed to the terrier.

'That dog, the smaller one, I believe that it is your dog. Is that correct, sir?'

Slavoj had listened closely to each word that had been spoken to him but, still, wasn't sure what had been said. And more importantly, he wasn't sure how he should reply. He looked down at the dogs as they continued to wrestle with each other on the grass.

The man pointed to the terrier.

'This animal. We have had complaints about this

animal. I am from the Housing Authority, sir, and as you would realise, under the written terms of your tenancy agreement, you are unable to keep an animal in your housing unit.'

He walked towards the dog. Both dogs stopped playing and momentarily looked up with bemusement before returning to their game.

'This dog has to go. It will be removed from the estate.'

Slavoj knew enough of what was being said to raise his hand in protest. He was about to speak when the old man stood up from the bench.

'This dog is going nowhere, mate. This is my dog. You'll be taking it nowhere.'

Both Slavoj and the man in the suit stared at the old man.

'Your dog? This cannot be your dog, sir. We have had several complaints about this particular dog. It belonged to an elderly tenant from this estate, since deceased, and then this tenant' — he pointed at Slavoj — 'and then this tenant kept the dog in his housing unit. I have just spoken with one of our staff members here on the estate and he has confirmed that this animal is that same animal. I have just now contacted the local ranger and he is on his way here to remove the dog and place it in a secure shelter until it can be processed. Sir.'

The old man removed his hat. Slavoj took a step back as he began to wave his hands around.

'Nobody, no fucking ranger, no Housing Authority,

no one is taking this dog away, not anywhere. He's my dog. He's always been my dog and you're not taking him anywhere.'

The man from the Housing Authority looked down at the terrier.

'Your dog? Who are you, sir? Are you a tenant? What is your name?' He looked at the dog again. 'And what is the name of your dog?'

The old man did not miss a beat.

'Don't worry about my name, sonny. I don't have to give you my name. I'm no tenant of yours. I don't live on the estate. Anyway, what's your name, you officious prick?'

'Thompson. I am Richard Thompson. Community Liaison. And I have authority here.' He pointed to the terrier. 'Now, if this is your dog, what is its name?'

The old man looked down at the terrier.

'Jez. Jezebel. That's his name.'

It was the larger dog that pricked its ears in recognition. It jumped up from the grass and ran to the feet of the old man, who tried in vain to palm the dog away.

Thompson looked down at Slavoj's terrier as it rolled onto its back. He pointed to the dog's testicles.

'This dog, this dog is a male. And you just called it Jezebel. This is not your dog.'

Slavoj tried in vain to follow the increasingly confusing conversation as the old man fired back.

'Well, Jez, Jezebel. It's all the fucking same, mate.

Don't you try telling me this is not my dog. I named
him after Alex Jesaulenko. You know, Jezza? Carlton?
Number twenty-five? The 1970 Grand Final? That
mark, over the top of Jerker Jenkins?'

The larger dog continued to sit at the old man's
feet. It barked up at him each time it heard its name.

Slavoj understood none of the old man's ramblings.
And if the representative of the Housing Authority did,
his contorted face gave nothing away.

'Jezebel — that's the wife's doing. She spoiled him,
doted over him. She's gone now. Me and Jez, we miss
her. Well, she used to sit on the couch with him of a
night, tickle that dog on the tummy and whisper to
him, "Love you, Jez, love you, my Jezebel." The name
just stuck. You know, like the song, 'A Boy Named Sue'
— "My name is Sue, how do you do?" Should have
called him Teddy maybe, Teddy Hopkins, to avoid all the
confusion. You know Teddy Hopkins, of course? Kicked
four goals in the second half and won the game for us.'

Thompson turned to Slavoj.

'This is not your dog? Is this man correct? Is this
your animal or is it not?'

Slavoj did not know what he should say. He
watched as the old man ambled across to the terrier. He
leaned forward and began to stroke the dog's stomach as
the larger dog nudged at his hand for attention. Slavoj
looked back at Thompson, who was obviously awaiting
an answer from him. He stumbled over his reply.

'Jezzi … Jezzi … twinny fire … Tiddy Hipkin …

him own.'

The old man came to Slavoj's rescue again. He was nursing the terrier in his arms and cooing to it repeatedly, 'Jezza, Jezza.'

He moved in closer to Richard Thompson. Although he was quite elderly the man had presence.

'You're all done here, mate. I've got to get my dogs home for a feed.' He then looked him in the eye. 'I said we're done here, aren't we, mate?'

Thompson took several steps back from the two men. 'This is Housing Authority property. And, as you are not a tenant, you are not to enter the estate, with or without your animals.'

He looked at the terrier as it enjoyed being cradled in the arms of the old man. 'That is, of course, if, as you claim, this is your dog.'

He then looked across at Slavoj one last time before storming off. The old man waited until he had disappeared before kneeling down and whispering in the ear of his own dog.

'Come on, Jezebel, my beauty. Let's go home for some lunch.'

The dog affectionately licked his hand. The man then turned to Slavoj.

'I live just here, in the side street. We best keep the little fella of yours at my place for a bit.'

He nodded in the direction of the man from the Housing Authority.

'This arsehole, Richard fucking Thompson, or

whatever his name is, will be lurking around for a bit yet. He's got a sniff and thinks he's onto something. Me and Jez, we can look after him for you. They can keep each other company.'

Slavoj ran the words 'arsehole' and 'Richard fucking Thompson' over and over in his head as the old man continued.

'It might be best if you keep a low profile, yourself. You hungry? Why don't you come home with us for a feed?'

The old man lifted his hand to his mouth and simulated a chewing action.

'Come home with us, you and the dog. I'll put lunch on. Celebrate a win over the Authority. Fuck 'em, hey?'

Between the clearer fragments of the old man's words and his action, Slavoj understood that the man was inviting him to share a meal. He looked down at the two dogs as they nuzzled against each other.

'Yes. I come. Thank you.'

'Don't thank me. Jez and me, we'd be happy for the company. And the feed — it's just meat and potatoes. It'll fill you up though, don't worry about that. We love our meat and potatoes, me and Jezebel. You look like you could use a good feed. You and the dog, both.'

The two men, with their dogs at their feet, walked across the estate towards the side street.

The old man turned to Slavoj and laughed.

'Tiddy? Tiddy Hipkin?' He looked down at the

terrier. 'Tiddy? Not a bad name for the dog. What do you think? Come on, Tiddy. Let's go home.'

# Gifted

I cupped a hand to the side of my face and squinted through the window into Ray's front room. Light flickered from the television set but I had learned not to take this as a sign that he was at home, as Ray usually left the set running day and night. Fortunately the sound had gone on his old TV months ago, so the neighbours had stopped complaining about the noise coming from the downstairs flat when they were trying to sleep.

I knocked at the window and listened for a response from inside, even if only the sound of Ray's slippered feet scuffling into a hiding place in his bedroom so he wouldn't have to answer the door. He did that often. I was nursing his twenty-fifth birthday present under my arm. When he didn't answer my second knock at the window I put the present on the ground between my feet, wrapped both hands around my mouth and yelled.

'Ray. Ray. Are you there?'

I felt a little stupid, standing at his window and screaming his name. It was a childhood habit, of calling him home of a night when he went drifting, which he did whenever he could escape the house. My mother would order me to go find him. I remember walking out the front door and screaming his name down the centre of the street, then waiting for him to come running out of a back lane or some kid's side gate with that vague look on his face, as if he was innocent of any wrong-doing.

As I continued to call out his name, the front door of the flat directly above his opened. It was the one where the tenants had complained about the noise. The creaking of the door was followed by the sound of footsteps out on the landing. I looked up to see a young girl, about fourteen or fifteen years old maybe, poking her head over the balcony and looking down at me. She moved back and forward a couple of times when she spotted me looking back up at her, before resting her chin on the steel railing and watching me closely through a mop of straw hair that fell across her freckled face.

'He's not in, you know. We saw him go off about half an hour ago. Leaves the same time every day. Gets back at the same time too. Except on weekends when he can go off for hours and hours. I reckon he'll be a little while yet. He gets back just before the Midday Movie comes on. We hear him at the gate. My mum, you know what she says when she hears him coming back? She says, "There he is, he's back." She's always saying that, my mum is.'

I looked at my watch. Ray was probably at morning mass right now. I'd forgotten that he attended eleven o'clock mass, seven days a week, without fail. I didn't want to look up again but could feel the girl watching me. I didn't want to get stuck in a conversation with her either but thanked her, just the same, for her information.

'That's all right,' she yelled back down to me. 'I seen him leaving from our kitchen window when I was making my mum a cup of tea. She's sick, she's a bit … well, she's sick, so I'm off school looking after her.'

The girl took a packet of cigarettes from her pocket and lit up.

'You want one? I can throw them down to you if you want one, and you can just chuck them back to me. You want a smoke?'

She went on chatting without waiting for a reply from me.

'You know, he only had his sandals on. Freezing cold and he's got no shoes on. Bare feet and sandals. He always does that. He was only wearing a T-shirt, too. No jumper, no jacket or nothing to keep him warm. Why's he do that, you reckon? Go out in the cold like that? Do you know him? You look a bit like him. Are you related to him or something?'

She stopped talking just long enough to catch her

breath before taking another drag on the cigarette.

'Is he all right? You know, I mean, all right? My mum says he must be off the planet or something. You know last week I was watching him from the kitchen window, I was looking down the lane, up to the yard behind Jackson's foundry, when he come along the lane with both arms loaded up with junk mail. I called to mum, to stop looking at the TV for a couple of minutes and get up from the couch and come over to the window for a look. "Look at him," I said to her. Well, she looked out of our window at him and just laughed — "mad bastard," she called him. That's what she said. I seen him another time pulling junk mail out of all the letterboxes along Wellington Street. Mail that had already been delivered. Brought it home with him, the lot, in a big black plastic bag. He must have raided every letterbox from here to Victoria Parade.'

She took another puff on the cigarette, lifted her head and blew the smoke into a rapidly darkening sky.

'What do you think of that? Why would he do that, do you reckon? Junk mail? It's just junk, isn't it? That's why they call it junk, don't they? Because nobody really wants it, isn't that it?'

I felt desperate to get away from the block of flats. There was no certainty that Ray would return any time soon. As the young girl from the upstairs flat had reminded me, he had a habit of walking the streets for hours on end, pacing out mile after mile. Ray could turn up anywhere.

One Friday afternoon about six months ago, a second cousin on my father's side of the family, Claudie, was delivering a load of firewood out near the old quarry in Brunswick when he saw Ray marching along the cyclone wire fence that bounded the quarry. Claude tooted to Ray and pulled over to the side of the road to have a talk to him.

'What are you doing, Ray, so far from home?' he'd laughed, as he wound down the passenger side window. Ray kept on walking as if he didn't recognise one of his own relations.

'Wait a minute, will you kid?' Claude called out to him.

'I'm walking,' Ray called back to him without as much as breaking his stride, let alone stopping to talk.

The best solution would be for me to leave the birthday gift in the utility cupboard on the verandah and go home and call him later. He didn't answer the telephone any more often than he did the front door but I could at least leave a message on his machine for him, to let him know where he could find his birthday present. I wouldn't have to talk to him either. I could simply leave him a happy birthday message and avoid the awkwardness that dominated any conversation between us.

Just as I had decided to desert the front porch a clap of thunder exploded above my head. It sounded like a bomb had gone off in the street. A sudden downpour of rain followed the thunderclap. I heard the door to the upstairs flat slam shut as the teenage girl retreated. I huddled under a concrete awning above Ray's front door and looked into the rain. I wouldn't be going anywhere in a hurry unless I was prepared to get soaking wet.

I turned a large, empty terra cotta pot upside down, pushed it into the sheltered corner of the verandah with the toe of my shoe, and sat down and watched as the rain flooded Ray's small front yard. Holding the gift in my hands, I looked down into a pattern of what were supposed to be party balloons, I guessed. Their thin, elongated shapes gave the appearance of condoms — perhaps they were supposed to resemble party condoms?

Inside the parcel were three T-shirts, each plain coloured — white, grey and black. Ray wore only T-shirts, and no jumpers or jacket, regardless of the weather. He refused anything else as a birthday or Christmas present. Nor would he accept bright colours or stripes, even if the gift was a T-shirt.

One year, desperately worried that he was sure to catch pneumonia that coming winter, my mother bought him three checked flannel shirts for his birthday, hoping he might wear them on a cold day.

'Won't fit,' he whispered as he placed the shirts on her kitchen table, without as much as removing them from the cellophane wrapping.

She had looked over at me anxiously as I sat on the couch nursing my, then infant, son Joshua. It was obvious that she was upset and wanted me to help her persuade Ray to wear the shirts. I could do no more than shrug my shoulders in resignation, knowing well that Ray could never be talked into anything he didn't want to do. She tried anyway.

'But Ray, you haven't even put one on,' she pleaded. 'They're your size, love, Small Men's.'

I heard footsteps at the front gate and then it opened. It was Ray. He watched me closely but didn't say a word. Then he pulled a face of disappointment that he showed any time his private world was violated. I moved away from the front door as he fumbled with his keys. The girl upstairs was right. Ray was standing on the doormat in a pair of worn-out, thin soled rubber sandals and wearing his regulation grey pants and a dark T-shirt that clung to his prematurely stooping frame.

Although he attempted to conceal it from me I also noticed that he had a pile of junk mail under one arm. He opened the door and went inside. He let the screen door slam against my arm as I followed him inside.

The front room was as neat as I had remembered it; sparsely furnished, with everything in its place. Ray didn't like to lose things. The only potential disorder in the room was provided by Ray's homemade bookshelves. His efforts to build them had progressively covered most of the available space along one wall of the lounge room as Ray brought more and more books home from charity shops.

The bookshelves were built from disassembled timber pallets that Ray retrieved from the loading bay behind the foundry at the end of the lane. He had always been good with his hands. He could make just about anything when he was a kid. Billy-carts, fighter planes, and his favourite, intricately designed model houses that he created from little more than ice cream sticks, matchboxes and cigarette packets.

'Who taught you to do that?' one of my mother's boyfriends asked Ray one night, in a vain attempt to get friendly with us as he pored over one of Ray's model towns sitting on the coffee table. Ray wouldn't answer him. He wouldn't look at him either.

Ray hadn't learned to make the model town from anyone. He was self-taught. He would sit patiently at the kitchen table of a night, building models copied from the paintings and photographs he saw in magazines and books.

I looked across to the wall behind Ray, wondering when the day would come that the gravity-defying structure of ramshackle shelving, laden with his books, would inevitably collapse into the room. For whatever reason he had built the shelves with none of the precision and care that had been his childhood trademark.

While I had been looking at the shelves he stood impatiently in the centre of the room with his hands resting tensely on his hips. He always expected any visitor to his flat to leave, more or less from the moment they walked inside the front door. Water dripped from his hair and clothing, down his legs and onto his feet, before running under the soles of his sandals and onto the threadbare carpet.

'Get a towel, Ray, and dry yourself off,' I tried ordering him. 'Change your wet clothes. You'll catch a cold or something.'

Preoccupied with thoughts of his own he ignored me.

'You got any change?' he said, holding out a hand.

'Change for what, Ray?'

'Just change.'

'What do you mean, just change? Money, you mean? You want money for something?'

'No. Change for the plate.'

'The plate? What plate?'

Unsure of what he was talking about, I looked around for a plate. He closely watched me as he clenched his hands together.

'The plate,' he tried explaining, obviously frustrated by what he regarded as my stupidity, 'for the church. The donation.'

I suddenly realised what he was talking about but now it was my turn to ignore the question. I handed him the gift.

'Happy birthday, Ray.'

He nursed the gift in his hands as he gently massaged the wrapping paper with the insides of his thumbs.

'Colours.'

Yet again, I had no idea what he was talking about.

'What?'

'Colours,' he said, holding up the gift.

'Don't just look at it, Ray. Open it up. The present. It's for you.'

He ripped the parcel apart and glanced at the T-shirts before dumping them on the couch. He held the gift paper in his hands. I felt around in the side pocket of my jacket for his birthday card.

'Here. I got the kids to sign it. Josh drew a picture of himself on the back of the card for you. Here, have a look.'

He let the wrapping paper fall to the ground as he snatched the envelope from me. He held it in his hand, running his fingers across its parchment surface and the six-year-old scripted, 'RAY!'

'Open it, Ray, will you?' Please?'

But he wouldn't. He looked down at the envelope and watched his own fingertips as they traced his name on surface of the paper.

I watched with increasing frustration before snatching the envelope from him and tearing it open. I let the paper fall to the floor. It landed next to the wrapping paper. Angrily, I shoved the opened card in his face.

'Read it, Ray. Read the birthday card, will you?'

He wouldn't even look at it. His eyes were fixed on the floor. He bent down and picked up the scraps of paper before turning around and walking through to the kitchen and into the bathroom, holding the torn envelope in one hand and the wrapping paper in the other. He closed the bathroom door behind him.

I noticed that there was another birthday card sitting on one of the bookshelves. I walked over, picked it up and read it. It was from my mother and was addressed to 'Golden Boy.' Although Ray was a grown man, and had been for many years, she insisted on treating him as if he were still a child.

Alongside the card, in a cheap tin frame that had probably belonged to my grandmother, was a photograph of Ray, taken when he was about twelve years old. He has a head of luscious curls, wide brown eyes and a beautiful smile. I picked up the picture frame. Studying the photograph more closely I could see the dark rings under his eyes and the look of apprehension and fear on his face, even back then when he was just a kid.

None of us had seen what was coming when he got sick. I often wondered if he had.

I returned the frame to the shelf and looked across the kitchen in the direction of the bathroom door. Ray was in hiding again. It would probably be best for both of us if I left. But seeing as it was his birthday I didn't want to go without at least saying goodbye. I walked through the kitchen and into the bathroom, switching off the television as I went.

When I got to the bathroom door I called his name and knocked a couple of times. I waited for a reply. When it didn't come I opened the door.

The room was stiflingly hot. A two-bar electric wall heater buzzed erratically above the towel cupboard.

Ray was standing over the bath and looking down into the tub. The torn birthday envelope and gift paper were partially submerged in a sea of grey sludge. At the end of the bath, leaning against the glass door of the shower recess, were two neat stacks of paper, comprising junk mail and old newspapers. Both stacks reached close to the ceiling. A third tower of paper lurked behind the shower recess. Ray and I looked down into the bath together as the envelope sunk slowly into the quagmire and disappeared.

I looked around the bathroom. Yet another stack of paper stood behind the door. On the laminex top of the towel cupboard, sitting directly below the heater, were two rows of cars — model cars fashioned from paper mache. They looked both grotesquely alien and immediately familiar. Although I hadn't seen it for many years, I immediately recognised that these almost identical models were replicas of a model Morris Minor that Ray had won in a lucky dip at the school fete one year, when he was about eight or nine-years-old. He had treasured the car from the day be brought it home and wouldn't let me touch it, let alone play with it.

I remembered how shattered Ray had been when he left the model car behind on the tram we rode home from the city, after we'd been to see the film, *Little Big Man*. It took months for him to get over it. I'd really enjoyed the movie and wanted to talk about it when we got home but Ray wouldn't shut up about his car. He wanted our mother to ring the Tramways Board and find out if anyone had handed the car in. She wouldn't do it and when he continued nagging her about it, she became furious with him.

'Raymond, it's just a tin car. A cheap tin car. Some poor kid who hasn't got much probably picked it up and put it in his pocket.'

'Ring the police then,' he demanded. 'Somebody has stolen my car.'

He was still upset about the lost car later that night when we were in bed. I tried cheering him up by playing the old Indian chief from the movie.

'Today is not a good day to die, Ray,' I called out to him as I lay on my back.

'I just want my car,' he whispered back.

Studying the drying models more closely I noticed that each of them was in fact slightly different, in shape, colour and texture. I could make out faded water-damaged images on the car chassis, along with bold newspaper headline letters or the splices of words across bonnets, roofs, and even the hubcaps:

'… OWARD NOT SOR …'

I could hardly believe what I was looking at and couldn't contain my excitement.

'Ray, these are amazing. I mean, truly amazing. What made you think of the Morris Minor?'

I moved to pick up one of the cars, before noticing that they were not quite dry. I pulled my hand away. Without responding to my question Ray rushed out of the bathroom.

I could hear him moving around his bedroom. I walked out into the hallway and stood in the doorway of his bedroom before hesitating and walking away, back into the lounge. I heard the front gate opening. It was probably my mother. She came over to the flat about every second day to clean it for him.

Ray came back into the front room. He had a black plastic bag slung over his shoulder, bulging with whatever was inside it. I presumed it was more junk mail. He was holding a model car in his hand. It had been painted. It was, not surprisingly, similar in colour to his original model, baby blue. Ray presented the car to me.

'Here. I made this for you.'

I took the car gently in my hands. I was genuinely touched by Ray's craftsmanship and his generosity. I also felt a sudden pang of guilt, thinking that while I had resented having to spend just a few minutes with him on his birthday, he had dedicated so much of his time recreating the lost treasure of his childhood — and for me, I thought.

Someone knocked at the door. Ray looked over to it and then down to the model car in my hands. It was obvious that he had no intention of answering the door, so I walked over and opened it.

A man was standing in the doorway. He sported a slicked back 1950s hairdo. It was streaked with flecks of grey. He was wearing a brown pin-striped suit, that looked a couple of sizes too small for him, and a loud floral tie. He waved a fan of glossy brochures teasingly in my direction.

'Afternoon, afternoon, sir. Well, it's a little damp underfoot, yes, hey, yes? Now, let's see, yes? I am here this afternoon on behalf of the …'

I was holding the door strategically ajar and could feel Ray's wheezing breath on the back of my neck. He pushed me to one side, grabbed the handle of the door and swung it open. He leaned across the doorway and with the one swift movement snatched the brochures from the salesman's hand and replaced them with another of his model cars, which he produced like a rabbit from a hat out of the black garbage bag.

'Here. I made this for you.'

I stood in the doorway with my paper mache model car in my hand. The startled salesman looked down at his own car, his shock quickly melting away into joy and an immediate sense of attachment to the model car. Ray stepped between the two of us, carrying the garbage bag over his shoulder. He rushed out into the street. It was still raining heavily. Oblivious as ever to the weather, Ray looked up at the grey sky and smiled as the raindrops bounced off his forehead.

I closed the front door behind me and followed him into the street, leaving the salesman on the doormat immobilised as he studied his Morris Minor. The girl from upstairs was standing alongside the row of letterboxes. She had a red parka draped over her head as she dug one hand into her mailbox while holding a lit cigarette in the other.

Ray reached into the garbage bag and pulled out another powder blue car. He tapped the girl on the shoulder.

'Here. It's my birthday today. I made this for you.'

He stopped and looked at the sign above the letterboxes and ran his hand across the letters: NO JUNK MAIL. He carefully placed a model car on the top of each of the letterboxes before heading along the footpath in the pouring rain. He stopped for a moment in front of the letterbox of each house along the street and reached into his bag of gifts.

The salesman and the girl in the red parka and I stood on the footpath together, with our Morris Minors, watching Ray as he delivered his gifts to each address. The girl carefully placed the car in a pocket of her parka to protect it from the weather.

'He's like that fella in the movie, isn't he?'

'What movie?' I asked her.

'You know, *Rain Man*, he's like that. Can he add up too? You know, numbers, really fast. Maybe he could help me with my homework?'

# Made to Measure

Late in the winter, when my father would normally be busy with customers, he pulled down the blind in his shop window, locked the door, came home and climbed into bed. He stayed there for weeks and when he did get up he got no further than the bathroom, where I would hear him dry-retch into the toilet bowl. We had little contact with each other beyond him handing me money each time I complained that I was hungry. I lived on potato chips, sweet biscuits, and my all time favourite lollies — raspberries.

The day before my tenth birthday I sat at the kitchen table with a packet of Teddy Bear biscuits and studied the calendar pinned to the back of the door leading out into the yard. There was only one day to go, until the circled number sixteen.

On the morning of my birthday I got out of bed

early and raced into the kitchen. My birthday present was usually waiting for me on the kitchen table. But on this day there was nothing, not even a card. I walked through the darkened hallway to my father's bedroom. The door was open and I could see him lying on his back, on top of the bed, with his arms folded across his chest. He reminded me of a photograph that I had once seen in a *National Geographic* magazine at the barbershop. It was of a dead man in a coffin in a village.

I took a couple of steps into the room to see if my father was breathing. He is dead, I thought.

A sense of panic began to rise through my body when he suddenly opened his eyes and stared across the room at me. My heart jumped in my chest and I grabbed at the front of my pyjama top, as if to stop it escaping. I wanted to ask him what we'd be doing for my birthday but I was too frightened to talk. He looked at me but didn't say a word. I turned around and ran back through the kitchen into the yard.

I picked up a handful of apricot stones from under the tree and began throwing them at the birds perched along our back fence. If my father saw me doing this he would have told me off. He loved birds and encouraged them into the garden with the feeder that he had built for them.

But the birds had nothing to fear from me. They flew away before I could get near them with my wayward shooting.

A spider had spun its web in the space between

the downpipe and the brick wall of our garage. I broke one of my father's tomato stakes in half and stabbed at the web with the jagged end of one half of the stake, hunting for the spider. It must have abandoned the web and I couldn't find it.

I searched the yard some more until I came across an ant nest behind the garage. I started poking around with my broken stake and had almost destroyed the nest before I spotted the leather football lying in the grass in the back corner. I picked it up and brushed away a fat juicy snail that had been crawling over its worn leather. The slimy trail left behind by the snail ran across the name SHERRIN.

The ball would have come over the fence from one of the backyards in the next street. I had no idea who it belonged to, so I decided to keep it. I kicked the ball around the yard, using the garage door as the goals. By the time I had worn myself out and lay on my back on the grass I had kicked six goals.

I heard the screen door slam shut. I looked up, surprised to see my father. He was wearing a clean white shirt, neatly pressed trousers and a pair of black leather shoes. I could smell the shoe polish. His hair was neatly combed and he had shaved.

He stopped in front of me and shuffled awkwardly from foot to foot. It was then that I noticed that he had his measuring tape draped around his shoulders. He looked just the way he did when he was at the tailor shop where he fitted men for the suits they needed for weddings or funerals.

He squatted down alongside me and began to speak slowly.

'I'm sorry, Michael, for missing your birthday. I ...' His voice trailed away.

He stood up and removed the measuring tape from around his neck. He held the tape in one hand, running it between his thumb and finger with the other hand. He looked down at the toe of one of his polished shoes. It was smudged with a crust of soil from the garden. He knelt down again and brushed the dirt away, watching me closely as he did. Then he leaned across and touched me on the side of the leg.

'Come into the kitchen.'

I walked behind him with fresh hope. Maybe he was going to give me a birthday present after all? As he searched through the cupboards and drawers I began to convince myself that he had hidden my present and was now about to surprise me.

I watched him closely as he took a brown paper bag from one of one of the drawers and laid it on the kitchen table. He smoothed creases in the paper with the palm of his hand. He then picked up a lead pencil and sharpened it to a point with a small wooden-handled knife

'So, you're ten today, Michael. Double figures. It wasn't too long after my tenth birthday that I realised I was going to grow up and become a man.' He laughed gently. 'Funny that, not knowing until then that I would one day become a man.'

'It gave me the shock of my life, discovering that I would one day grow up, like the older kids riding their bikes no hands down Federation Hill. Or like the teenage boys smoking cigarettes out front of the local pictures, where my old man, your grandfather, worked. Or worse, to think that one day I might end up like one of the workers hunched over their enormous shovels, busting their guts, at the foundry.'

He coughed a couple of times before going on. His voice became very tender but he measured his words deliberately and spoke with careful precision.

'I wanted to stay small. Just stay as a kid. And until then, when I was about your age, I had always assumed I would.'

He looked down at the now finely sharpened pencil point and motioned me toward him. He put the end of the pencil in his mouth and placed a hand on each of my shoulders. When he was satisfied with my posture he hung the tape from his left hand and lightly wrapped his right hand around my wrist as he guided my arm toward the horizontal position.

'Keep it there, keep it there,' he whispered softly as he released his grip.

He measured the length from my wrist to the point of my shoulder. Then he placed the tape on the kitchen table, took the pencil from his mouth and neatly recorded the measurement at the top of a column on the piece of brown paper. He proceeded to measure other parts of my body, manoeuvring me with the delicate pressure of only his palms and fingertips.

I had seen him do the same thing many times at work in the shop. I would sit in the corner of the fitting room after school, reading a book or doing my homework while he discussed a groomsman's outfit with an awkward-looking and embarrassed factory worker. My father would circle these men with his measuring tape, touching them occasionally as he enquired about who was getting married or made small talk about family or football.

Sometimes I felt that I was watching grown men dance with each other.

I was puzzled as to why he was measuring me now but was also attracted to the neat row of figures gradually filling the column that my father had drawn on the brown paper bag. He wrapped the tape around my waist and drew it together like a trouser belt before bending down and squinting at the precise lines and numbers woven into its cloth.

'Why are we doing this, Dad?' I asked him.

He said nothing as he concentrated on recording another set of measurements on the paper. When he had completed the neat column he continued with his story.

'I will never forget my first year at primary school. I was tiny, the smallest kid in school that year. We used to have to stand in a straight line, in the schoolyard outside the classroom; the tallest to shortest, for roll call, boys and girls together. I was even shorter than any of the girls.'

He stopped talking as he took a step back, gently turned me to my side and studied my profile.

'There I stood, on the end of the line. Our teacher that year, I can't remember his name, but he was real tall. Towered over me like a giant. He had this raincoat, and he wore it all the time, even when the sun was out. Even on hot days. He put me in a desk right up the front, so I wouldn't disappear, he said.'

After he had finished measuring me with the tape my father led me over to the kitchen doorway and instructed me to stand to attention against the doorframe. He took the breadknife from the drying rack on the kitchen sink, slid its cold metal over the top of my head and dug it into the wooden architrave of the doorway until it had made its mark in the fresh paintwork. He asked me to hold one edge of the tape against the base of the doorway at floor level while he ran the tape back up along the architrave so that he could measure my height.

'To tell you the truth, I always hated school,' he went on. 'The bigger kids were always picking on me. Schools did nothing about bullying in the schoolyard in those days. You had to cope for yourself. But I couldn't cope. So one day, after my mother had left me at the school gate, I decided I was going to nick off. I was going to run away from school and never go back. And I did. When no one was watching me I sped out of the gate, down the street, and around the corner. But I ran straight into my mum, your grandmother. She was on her way to the shops. Jesus, she was mad at me.

'She started asking me lots of questions. "What's going on? You being chased? You in trouble?"

'I'm too small,' I cried to her. 'I'm too small.'

"Too small? What do you mean, too small? For what?"

'Too small for school …'

My father sat down at the kitchen table and studied the figures. It was as if he wanted to extract something more from the numbers. A teardrop fell from his cheek and onto the paper bag. As he tried wiping it away he smudged some of his pencilled numbers.

We sat at that table together, perfectly still except for our shared breathing.

When he finally did move again it was to retrieve his lead pencil, which had rolled off the tabletop. He bent down, picked up the pencil and checked the point to see if it had been broken in the fall. The pencil had not broken but he began to resharpen it with his knife just the same.

'My mother let me stay home that day, but she ordered me back to school the next morning.'

He folded the brown paper bag into a neat square before slipping it into the breast pocket of his shirt.

'I gave up running away from school after that. I

realised that I had no choice but to get used to it. And when that happened. I just sort of sprang up, overnight. Started to grow.'

He shook his head and chuckled to himself as he thought about what he had just said.

I looked around the bare walls of the kitchen. After we moved here my mother had framed several magazine posters of movie stars and put them on the walls of the kitchen. They were gone, now. There was nothing to look at but the calendar hanging from the wall. I began to fidget. One of my feet kicked the leg of my father's chair.

# The Ward

Beds lined each side of the ward separated by an aisle little wider than a hospital trolley. It could get pretty hectic and most staff avoided working there if they could. But I liked the ward — it was always busy and time passed quickly. I was also taken by the view at the far end of the ward. A large window overlooked the park opposite the hospital, while the city skyline sat beyond a line of elm trees along the park's boundary.

At around three or four in the morning, when even the most restless patients managed some sleep, I would stand at the window and look across to one of the glass towers of the city and search for signs of movement. Sometimes I would locate a worker at a desk, their face lit by the white light of a computer screen.

I took over from Jenny at the change of shift. She had retired from nursing years ago but came back after her husband, a QC and hobby farmer, suffered a stroke. Jenny was an assertive but calm influence on the ward.

'You've got a new fella just come in, in bed seven. A Mr Callan. He's got theatre in the morning. He's a bit anxious. And old Joe across the way has been quiet all afternoon. Look in on him. He might be hungry.'

As I made my way through the ward I glanced across to a teenage boy, Sean, in bed five. Three days earlier he had been moved across from Intensive Care. His mother had dragged a chair to the head of the bed, sat down and held his hand. She had hardly moved since.

The metal rail at the foot of his bed was draped in an autographed Collingwood football jumper and matching scarf. Sean was a member of the Collingwood Cheer Squad and two of the club's players had visited him the previous day. After their visit he had invited me to watch the Carlton–Collingwood game with him on the weekend.

As I passed the bed his mother smiled at me. She looked weary but relieved. Anyone looking at the boy would be horrified. His partially shaved skull had been knitted together with steel clips following an operation to relieve pressure on his brain, caused by bleeding. A drunk driver had knocked him off his bicycle on the way home from football training. He was unconscious when he arrived at hospital and was rushed to surgery.

Joe Pike was in bed eight, behind a curtain drawn around his bed. I opened the curtain slightly and stuck my head in to check in on him. His blanket had fallen to the floor and he was curled in a ball on his bed, facing the window. In his candy-striped pyjamas, he looked more like a young boy than an old man. A pile of books sat on the side table next to his bed, while photographs of grandchildren and get well cards, were posted on the wall above the bed.

Joe had been on the ward for several weeks and had been due to move to a hospice over a week ago, until the duty social worker managed to persuade the administration to let him stay. He lived with his wife, a daily visitor, within walking distance from the hospital. When she was told that the time had come for him to move to the hospice, in the eastern suburbs, Mrs Pike burst into tears, worried that she would be unable to visit him.

I picked up the blanket and covered him. He opened his eyes and looked up at me, a little confused. I placed a hand on his shoulder.

'I'll be back soon, Joe. We'll have a wash, and something to eat.'

He smiled and nodded his head.

I closed the curtain, moved across the aisle, stood at the foot of bed seven and waited for the man lying on the bed to look up at me. He was resting on his side, concentrating on a glossy magazine, *Business Monthly*. He wore maroon silk pyjamas with cream pipping. Many public patients arrived at the hospital in flannelettes and worn-out Hush Puppies. Others didn't even bother with pyjamas, content to get around in a regulation tie-up gown with their arse showing to the world.

I took a quick look around the cubicle. A pair of leather slip-ons lay on the floor next to the bed, while some carefully arranged toiletries and two bottles of imported mineral water sat on the side table. Mr Callan's dinner tray, on a stand to one side of the bed, had not been touched.

I read the paperwork in his file. He was in for a hernia.

'Mr Callan? Ethan Callan,' I said, pointing to the prep sheet in the front of the file.

He continued reading the magazine. I spoke a little louder.

'Mr Callan?'

He looked up at me, placed the magazine on the side table, turned onto his back and put both hands behind his head.

'I'm Henry. Your nurse. You're having a hernia operation in the morning. I'll be looking after you tonight.'

I lifted the metal lid of his dinner plate. 'Roast beef and vegies. You haven't touched it, Ethan. You'll be fasting from midnight. You should get some food into you while you can.'

He stiffened. 'I'm not hungry.'

'Well, you will be if you don't eat this. Your next meal won't be until tomorrow night. You want this heated in the microwave?'

'No, thank you. I couldn't eat.'

I shrugged my shoulders. He looked wound up, most likely pre–op nerves.

'Okay then, Ethan. We need to take your blood pressure and temperature. I'll come back for the shave prep later on.'

He ran his hand across the side of his face and over the top of his bald scalp.

'What's that? A prep?'

'A shave prep, Ethan,' I explained. 'We have to shave the area in and around what we call the operational zone. But don't you worry. It will take just a few minutes.'

He moved his hand back down the side of his face and began tugging at his pyjama top. The top button popped open. He nervously fingered the buttonhole.

'I don't need a shave. I have no … no hair.'

It was true that he had no hair — well, none that I could see, at least. His face was clean-shaven, as was his head. As he continued to pull at the pyjama top a second button popped open, exposing his chest, which, I noticed, was also hairless.

'I don't have any *bodily* hair,' he emphasised.

I held up the prep slip.

'Sorry, Ethan, but before I can sign this off, I have to check.'

'Check?'

'Yes, check, down there.'

I checked. Mr Callan's body was completely hairless, like a child's.

Ethan didn't say a word while I took his pressure

and temperature. He didn't look at me either. He was staring at the neighbouring bed, at the side of Sean's skull. The stainless steel clips embedded in his head formed a perfect arc.

'You sure you won't try some food?' I asked a final time.

'No,' he answered quietly, as he continued looking at the boy.

When I returned to Joe's bed, he hadn't moved. He was usually washed of a night but, if he was sleeping, we left him be. I was about to leave his cubicle when he called out to me.

'Hey ya, son.'

I moved to the window side of the bed.

'Sorry, Joe. I thought you were asleep.'

He was looking out of the window toward the city skyline.

'You see that Henry? All those lights?'

I rested both hands on the windowsill.

'Yeah. It's a great view, isn't it Joe? People pay big money for that. Joe, you're a lucky man,' I added, before realising what I'd said.

When I looked apologetically at him he smiled.

'Oh, I'm lucky, all right. I always have been. One look at my wife, Ruby, would tell you that.'

Ruby arrived at the ward each morning, early enough to help Joe with his breakfast. She stayed for most of the day, reading to her husband as he drifted in and out of sleep.

'Yes. You are lucky, Joe.'


The day after his hernia operation I drew the curtain around Ethan's bed and checked the dressing around his wound. He was more talkative than when we had met. He told me he'd popped the hernia while moving an old refrigerator from of the kitchen of a house he'd just rented.

'I live on my own, Henry,' he told me. 'I should have left it until I could get someone to help me. But I've always been impatient,' he smirked. 'I tried dragging it out the room on my own. It was like wrestling a bear. I was giving it all I had when I felt a pain in my side, like someone had stuck a knife in me.'

I finished and pulled the curtain back. He looked across to Joe's bed. He was propped up on pillows and Ruby was sitting by the bed quietly reading to him. I was about to leave when Ethan asked me to wait.

'I suppose you're curious as to why I have no body hair?' he whispered, possibly worried that Joe or Ruby might overhear him.

'To be honest with you, not really, Ethan. Take a look around. There's plenty here to keep me curious.'

Whether I was interested or not Ethan was determined to share something with me.

'I was working on the floor of the stock market. I had been since I had left university. I was good at it, too. I made more in my first year than my father did as a bank manager.'

Ethan lifted his chest slightly. It was something he must have been proud of.

'But it was hard. Long hours. I started working longer hours, chasing markets. Hong Kong. Wall Street. It was about the same time I met my girlfriend, Mina. She was with one of the big traders, in futures. We were both working hard, but enjoying ourselves. Parties. Always the best restaurants. And then she shifted to nights, so she could concentrate on the European markets. She slept days. Or so I thought.'

Ethan stopped for a moment. I thought the story was over. But he took a deep breath, let out a sigh and went on.

'I was on the market floor one afternoon when my nose starting bleeding. It wouldn't stop — all the stress, I realised in hindsight.'

He pointed to the problem area by rubbing the tip of his nose.

'I had a shocking headache so I went home early. When I got there, to our apartment, and opened the door, I heard music playing. Coming from the bedroom. I pushed the door open and there they were, in our bed. To be truthful, I couldn't take my eyes off them. When she looked across the room at me she didn't seem at all surprised to see me standing there. And she didn't move. She just stared at me, from the bed, until I left the room.'

I took a step back when Ethan clenched a fist and

slammed it into his pillow.

'She was doing it in our fucking bed! And to our fucking song!' he hissed.

He had a confused look on his face, as if he was yet to comprehend what had happened to him. Ruby had stopped reading. She looked over at us.

'Look, I have to go, Ethan. Wash my hands.'

He appeared not to hear me.

'I didn't force her to leave, she packed her things that night and was gone. I worked longer hours, trying to keep myself busy, and my mind off what had happened. It worked for a while. But then the recession hit and …
I arrived at the office one morning to an email from my supervisor informing me that I had been sacked. His office was right next door to mine. He didn't even bother to knock on my door and tell me in person.'

He looked like he was about to cry.

'That's when I began to lose my hair. First I found clumps in my hairbrush, then in the shower, and even on my pillow when I woke of a morning. My doctor diagnosed a nervous condition. He asked me if I was stressed. Stressed! Eventually I was completely bald. Everywhere. And my hair has not come back.'

He was crying now. I drew the curtain around us.

'Ethan, you're due to be discharged tomorrow. Before you leave maybe you could have a chat to the social worker. Or the Chaplain. He's non-denominational. He's a good man.'

He looked offended.

'I don't need a priest.'

'He's not a priest. Just someone to talk to. Or the social worker. You could talk to her.'

He wiped his face with the sleeve of his pyjama top.

'No. I don't need to talk to anyone.'


I arrived for my shift the following afternoon and went to the locker room and changed into my uniform. As I was leaving the room I heard the door open on the service lift at the far end of the corridor. Two attendants from the hospital mortuary pushed a trolley into the lift. I watched the plump green body bag until the doors closed.

I could feel my heart beat rising. I was about to go into the ward when I was almost run over by Sean's mother pushing her son in a wheelchair. He was wearing his autographed football jumper. It was about two sizes too big for him.

'Sean, you're up and about?'

He smiled but couldn't get a word out before his mother interrupted.

'The doctor says it's fine. For a half hour, or so.' She looked over her shoulder to the doorway leading into the ward. 'He needs a break from this.'

I went straight to the nurse's station and looked up at the white board above the desk. It provided a brief summary of the condition of each patient. The current information for both bed seven and eight had just been posted. I didn't move for a minute or so before leaving the station and walking toward the other end of the ward.

Ethan was sitting in a chair next to his bed. He was wearing a dark suit and white open neck shirt. A leather overnight bag sat at his feet. We both looked across to the cubicle opposite. It was completely bare. The linen had been stripped from the bed and Joe's personal items had been removed.

'You're going home, then?'

'Yes. I'm just waiting for some paperwork. Then I can go, they said.'

He stood up and put his hand out, as if he wanted me to shake it. Then he removed it and put it back in his pocket. He looked once more over at Joe's empty bed.

'His wife, she asked me to thank you when you came on. For all you'd done for him, she asked me to tell you.' He pointed to the bag. 'She gave me a couple of books to read. Novels.'

'Novels?'

'Yeah. I haven't read a novel since high school.'

He took his hands out of his pockets, picked up his bag with one hand as he thrust the other toward me. He was determined that I shake it.

'So, thank you, Henry.'

I shook his hand.

'Thank you, Ethan. Can I give you some advice? You take it easy with that wound. No moving fridges around the house.'

I stood at the foot of Joe's bed for a few minutes and looked down at the mattress. The indentation of his body was still there. I rested the palm of my hand on the mattress. It felt warm. I turned and rested my elbows on the window sill as I looked out of the window. The silhouette of trees shifted in the breeze and, scattered among the buildings beyond, a handful of solitary people worked into the night.

# The Tern

For more than a year now my elderly neighbour, Jack, has been sorting through his life and getting rid of some of his stuff. We're not family. We've only known each other for a couple of years but a lot of what he has no further use for has come my way.

He began with hardback copies of books, *The Encyclopaedia of Australian Tractors* and *Tractors and Modern Agriculture*. He offered them to me one sunny morning as we were talking across the scraggy hedge of lavender that passes for the fence separating our properties.

Jack knows his tractors and loves talking about them. Had he been a contestant on the old *Mastermind* television quiz, tractors would surely have been his 'special subject'. He spent his working life selling tractors across Victoria in partnership with his identical twin brother, Ronnie. They set up the business together and a couple of years later married girls from their hometown — in the same church and on the same day.

They'd also planned to retire to a pair of neighbouring beach blocks on the west coast. But, just a few months before they were to quit the business, the truck Ronnie was driving was washed from a bridge during a flood while he was trying to cross a swollen river out the back of Colac. The battered wreck eventually turned up a few miles downstream from the scene of the accident but Ronnie's body was never found.

Even though he missed Ronnie greatly, Jack went ahead with his retirement plan just the same, while Ronnie's widow sold their block to 'some city type', as Jack referred to the lawyer who bought the block from her. Although the 'city type' built a house next door to Jack, he rarely visited it over the following years before putting it on the market.

I bought the house from the lawyer with the dream of fixing it up when I needed a break from writing the great Australian novel. But I've done little work on the house since moving in and have scratched out no more than a few paragraphs of bad writing.

In addition to his books on tractors Jack has also been handing his old tools across the hedge to me. To be honest they're as useful to me as the books on tractors. It's not that I don't appreciate his generosity, but I couldn't bang a nail straight to save myself.

Jack has taken great care of his tools. The oiled metal surfaces are rust free, while the wooden handles have been worn smooth by the years of use. I don't expect I will do anything with them but each offering, be it a shovel, a hammer or a variation on the basic hand saw, has been added to a growing collection I keep in the room behind the kitchen overlooking the back yard.

It is also the room where I do my writing. Or to be exact, it is where I am supposed to spend my day writing. I always begin what I refer to as my 'writing day' seated at my desk, armed with a strong cup of tea and some inspirational music. My 'writing music' as I optimistically refer to it. My working morning alternates between staring at the computer screen and then out of the window at an overgrown back garden that is badly in need of the attention I am unable to give it, as I am busy with my writing.

After an hour or so, sometimes less, I realise that today is not a good day to write. So I get up from my desk, leave the house and walk to the bottom of the garden. I slip through the gap in the fence and head for the beach

When I began my daily walks to the beach Jack was always alongside me. Actually it was Jack who showed me the secret pathway, hidden beneath a mass of tea-tree just over my back fence. And it was Jack who guided me along the pathway to the beach, where he shared a second secret with me.

On the morning of that first walk I had just given up on another writing session when Jack found me pacing around in my front garden. I was on a search, not for a story, but a humble sentence, or even a single word that might get me started.

'Hey ya, son,' he waved across the hedge to me.

Sure that there had to be something troubling a man beating a track into his yard, Jack walked around the hedge, blocked my path and asked if he could help. When I explained that I was reasonably certain that I had contracted writer's block he looked me in the eye, both puzzled and concerned.

'Writer's block?' he repeated to himself several times. 'Never heard of it. What is it?'

'Well, it's like having a problem that you can't sort out. Or an idea you're looking for. An idea with words. But words you can't find.'

Jack's eyes lit up, confident he had a solution.

'Well, you've got it half right, trying to work through your problem with a walk. I do that. Take a walk and sort the head out. But going round and round in circles? That's not good for you. You've got to walk in a straight line.'

He waved in the direction of the low hills behind our neighbouring homes.

'A straight line, son. A straight line.'

He coaxed me down to the bottom of his garden and pointed to a two-paling gap in the fence behind his shed.

'I've thought about putting a gate in here,' he explained to me as we climbed through the fence. 'It would be easier than doing this every morning. But to tell you the truth, it wouldn't be as much fun. Makes me feel like a bit of a kid.'

I could see a narrow track ahead of us, disappearing beneath a canopy of tea-tree. I walked behind Jack along a shaded track that rose sharply, reached a ridge, and then sloped gently down to the beach between sand hills and waves of golden grass.

He waited for me on the beach as I crossed a strip of sand littered with straps of leathery kelp. We took our time as we walked on, chatting and stopping occasionally to admire the dazzling colours in the rock pools, wedged tightly between the beach and the ocean. As he identified each species of fish weaving through the forests of seaweed I felt like a boy trailing joyously behind his father.

We had walked for maybe a half hour or so when Jack left the beach and headed into the long grass. He walked about thirty metres and then stopped. He nodded in the direction of a shallow depression in the ground.

'There it is,' he said, pointing to the spot we were both staring at. I had no idea what I was supposed to be looking for.

Jack's eyes widened as he pointed again.

'Well, what do you think, son?'

I looked again at the flattened bed of grass.

'What do I think about what?'

If he heard my question, he ignored it.

'Every summer, they come. Have been since I've had my place. And thousands of years before that, I'd reckon.'

'Who comes?'

'Not who, son. What. The Tern.'

He said those words — the Tern — quietly and calmly, like I should have known, without question, what it was he was referring to.

Jack turned around and started back along the beach. He surprised me by breaking into a jog. I ran after him. I wanted to know more about what it was that so excited him. He stopped at a wide shallow rock pool, rested his hands on his hips and took some deep breaths.

'The Arctic Tern,' he began explaining in between several gravelled coughs. 'It's a bird. A courageous bird. It comes right here, to this beach every summer, from the top of the world, from the Arctic Circle. More than twenty thousand miles it flies, to get here. And then later on in the year it flies back again. Same distance. Most people never get to see the bird because it spends so much of its life in the air.'

I looked across the ocean to the horizon in the distance and then up at the empty sky.

'Must be a big bird, Jack, if it's able to fly all that distance?'

'Na,' he scoffed. 'Wingspan's maybe a foot across, a bit more. And the bird itself,' Jack clenched his gnarled fist, 'not much bigger than this.'

I whistled with admiration.

'So you've seen it then? The bird?'

He looked at me and softened his face but said nothing more.

We headed home. Occasionally I looked over my shoulder to the clear morning sky.

'How do they get here, Jack? From the Arctic Circle?'

'They fly,' he laughed.

'But how? How do they know where they're going?' I stared out to the horizon. 'All that way.'

He stopped and grabbed hold of my arm. I was surprised by the strength of his grip.

'You're full of questions, aren't you, son? But that's good,' he smiled. 'They remember, son. That's how. It takes them months to get here. I read it up. Scientists have tracked that bird to every stop along the way. Same place every year, they stop. They never forget where they've been, or where they're heading. That's their secret. Never forget. Remember that yourself, son. Good lesson from a bird, that is.'

He gripped my arm again.

'And you know what else?'

I didn't have a clue.

His eyes glowed with joy.

'They live a long life, for a bird that is. More than twenty years they live, some of them. All that flying, you'd think it would wear them out. But it doesn't. All their strength comes from that flying. And another thing. Over all that time, they mate for life. They fly all over the world to the same place and the same mate, every year. What about that, hey?'

After we had slipped back through the fence Jack invited me into his garden shed.

'I've got something in here for you,' he said, winking at me cheekily.

His shed was an exercise in order. A vast supply of nails, screws, nuts and bolts were arranged in labelled glass jars along the back of a wooden workbench beneath a window looking onto the yard. His garden tools, shovels, rakes and picks of varying sizes, stood to attention along one wall, while his saws, hammers and drills hung from brackets above the garden tools.

There was not a power-tool in sight.

Odd lengths of wood, some of them 'rare finds' according to Jack, lay on a raised open rack across the back of the shed. And below the collection of wood a second shelf had been neatly stacked with several dozen tins of paints and varnishes.

'What are we looking for, Jack?' I wondered aloud, as he rummaged around the shed.

He looked up from a cardboard box marked ODDS AND ENDS in heavy lead pencil and answered simply, 'My binoculars.'

When he couldn't find them in the box, he left the shed and returned with a wooden ladder. He rested it against the back wall and directed the end of the ladder to the top shelf, where a kerosene heater, more cardboard boxes and an old suitcase sat.

As he tested the sturdiness of the ladder I offered my services.

'Can I help, Jack? Let me climb up there for you.'

He waved me away without a word as he put a foot on the bottom rung of the ladder. He climbed up to the shelf and moved one of the cardboard boxes aside to reach for a second box. The box cannoned into the suitcase. I jumped back as the case crashed to the floor.

'Shit,' Jack whispered to himself as he looked over his shoulder and down at the suitcase.

He searched through several more boxes before lifting a scuffed leather binocular case from one of them. He took the binoculars out of the case.

'Here they are.'

I stood at the bottom of the ladder as he passed the binoculars down to me. They were in immaculate condition — the dark metal, the chrome, the glass lenses. Each surface reflected the sunlight at the shed window.

He climbed down from the ladder and rested a hand on my shoulder.

'When he heads back this summer, the Tern, you'll be ready for him.'

I looked down at the glasses.

'But what does he look like? I can't tell one bird from another.'

Jack answered by handing me a book from a shelf above the workbench — *Migratory Birds of the World*. As I flicked through the pages he concentrated on the suitcase that had fallen to the floor. He picked it up by the handle and shook the case. I heard something rustling gently inside. I looked at Jack to see if he had heard it also.

'What have we got here?' he wondered aloud, shaking the case again.

He rested the case on the workbench, moved to unbuckle it and then hesitated for a moment before finally opening it. I moved closer to the workbench and looked down at the dazzling sequins sewn into the pure white fabric of what appeared to be a wedding dress.

Jack reached into the case and lifted the dress out. He nursed it in his arms like a newborn baby.

'This is my wife's wedding dress,' he explained. 'She's been gone more than ten years now.'

He slowly circled the room, holding the dress gently against his body, as if he were waltzing with it. When I saw that he had tears in his eyes I walked out into the garden, leaving him alone.

When Jack eventually came out of the shed he invited me into the house. We sat at a wooden table in the kitchen, sipping mugs of sweet tea. The only sound breaking the silence of the room were the birds nattering to each other in the tea-tree outside the kitchen window.

Jack looked into his mug and then across the table at me as he spoke.

'You know, we were married for more than forty-five years. We'd even started planning our fiftieth anniversary.'

He lifted the empty mug from the table and cradled it in his hands and the put it down again.

'Then she got sick. With the cancer.' He seemed to shiver with fear. 'There was a lot of pain, at the end.'

He stood up from the table, took our cups over to the sink, rinsed them under the tap and picked up the tea-towel.

'All those years on the road, travelling from town to town. I should have been home with her. It was only after I'd lost her that I worked it out. We'd spent more time away from each other, more nights in those years in separate beds, in separate towns, than where we should have been, at home and in each others arms.'

I felt I should say something. I wanted to tell Jack that I was sure they'd loved each other very much, and that their time together would more than have made up for the nights apart. But I couldn't say it. I felt that I didn't know him well enough to do so. And besides, we were men, so I said what is expected of men on such occasions.

'You were out there working hard, Jack, for both of you. I'm sure she would have understood.'

He looked around the room as he thought about what I had said.

'We both understood,' he finally answered. 'You're right there. But it changes nothing. Those nights apart add up to years of separation. Wasted years they are.'

It was early in Spring that I first noticed the change in Jack. I was at the mailbox one morning when he shouted out to me from across the hedge.

'Ron! Hey, Ronnie boy!'

He smiled and waved at me, before his expression changed and he quickly looked away. He seemed confused and embarrassed. I walked around the hedge. Jack was scuffing the ground with the toe of his boot as he studied a bare patch of grass in his lawn.

'I'll have to top-dress this and sow it, I reckon.'

'Jack. Are you okay?'

He would not look up at me.

'Yeah. I'm right, son. I was just thinking about something. Don't you mind me? I'm just an old fool.'

In the following weeks I had to return several of Jack's tools after he confided in me that he'd misplaced a hammer or saw.

'I don't want to be a nuisance but have you got one I can borrow for a few days?'

He also began to slow down and walked to the beach with me less often.

When I knocked at his door one morning in early summer, Jack didn't answer. That hadn't happened before. I made my way down to the gap in the back fence on my own, with the binocular case hanging from a leather strap around my neck. When I reached the ridge above the beach I took the glasses out of the case and scanned the horizon. There were plenty of birds around, seagulls mostly, but no sign of Jack's Arctic Tern.

If Jack had been with me he would have asked, 'Anything out there today?'

And after I'd replied, as I always did, 'Nothing this morning,' he would have become momentarily disappointed before lifting his spirits. 'Tomorrow. Maybe tomorrow.'

I walked down through the sand hills and along the beach to the spot where Jack had predicted the bird would eventually return. It wasn't there. When I turned for home I noticed someone on the beach in the distance, walking away from me. Although I was surprised to spot his wiry frame I was certain it was Jack. I lifted the glasses. He was heading for the surf beach.

I ran towards him calling, 'Jack! Jack!'

He didn't look around until I was almost alongside of him. He studied me closely, even a little suspiciously.

'Ronnie? Ronnie?' He took a step back. 'Ronnie Boy? Well, I'll be buggered. Where have you been all this time?'

I offered him an open hand.

'Sorry, Jack, but I missed you this morning. Must have slept in. Come on. Let's walk back to the house together.'

He looked further along the beach, to where some teenage boys were laying on a grass embankment above the surf beach. With their dark wetsuits glistening in the sun they resembled a colony of seals.

Jack turned and looked in the direction we had come from. He stared down at the sand, at the impression his footprints had made in the sand just a few minutes earlier. He followed their journey back along the beach as an incoming wave slid gently across the sand and swallowed them.

'Home?' He looked bewildered.

'Yeah. Home Jack. We should head back now.'

At that moment something fell into place for him. His look of confusion shifted to one of calmness, followed by a slight smile of recognition. He looked down at my open hand as if it were an unintended insult to his independence. He brushed me aside.

'Come on, son. I've got something to show you.'

Winter is about to arrive and Jack has not walked to the beach with me since that morning. A little over a week ago I was on the track, heading for the beach when a storm hit. As the heavy rain soaked through my woollen jumper and baggy track pants I thought about retreating to the house, or at least returning for a raincoat. I stopped for a moment before going on.

The low sky over the horizon was bruised with heavy weather, while the incoming rain, driven by a fierce southerly gale, stung my face. There seemed little point in bothering to remove the binoculars from their case but I took them out anyway and went through the motions of searching the horizon.

First I spotted a cargo ship, overladen with multi-coloured containers. The ship was being thrown around in the white-capped sea like a Lego model. It wasn't until I lifted the glasses to the sky above the ship that I caught a glimpse of a shadow against a cloud and then the dark smudged outline of a bird.

It was in my sights for just a few seconds before vanishing again. Although it was only a brief sighting I was convinced that it could only be the Tern. Perched on the ridge, I scanned the horizon for another half hour or more but did not see the bird again.

By the time I got back to the house I was wet to the bone and shivering with cold. I threw my clothes into the washer and jumped in the shower, enjoying the hot water. I dressed and left the house, running around the hedge to Jack's front yard. I knocked at his door several times but he didn't answer. I went back to the house and made myself a cup of tea, went into the lounge room and flipped through my CD collection until I found some writing music.

I sat at my desk surrounded by the musty smell of tractor books and the oiled surfaces of ancient metal tool and began to write:

*The Tern has a sharp blood-red beak and wears a black hood with a white cap. When the Tern grazes in the grasslands and low dunes, where it prepares its nest, its true beauty remains hidden beneath a covering of dull grey feathers. But when it lifts it wings in flight, particularly when gliding, which it does to conserve energy, the bird exposes its translucent mix of rich colouring. The Tern is a bird of strength and beauty.*

# Father's Day

The traffic on Sydney Road had ground to a halt and I was about to pull out from the kerb when I spotted my father standing in the rain on the footpath, across the street from where I was parked. Both his hair and the full beard he had grown since I'd last seen him were snow-white and dripping wet. He was wearing a ragged-looking red parka and seemed to have put on weight. He fumbled with the jacket and appeared to be having trouble buttoning it. A small stocky-looking dog was sitting at his feet. I hadn't seen it before either. It was as soaked as he was and didn't look at all happy.

I wound down the car window, tooted the horn and called out to him.

'Dad. Dad.'

If he heard me above the noise of the morning traffic he didn't bother looking my way, so I called out to him a couple more times and then held my hand down on the car horn. A woman sitting on a bench at the tram stop alongside the car put a finger in each ear and gave me a dirty look but he didn't respond at all.

The rain was coming in through the window, hitting me in the face. I wound the window back up, turned the key in the ignition and indicated to move into the traffic. As I waited on the generosity of any driver willing to offer me a few feet of road so I could join the Sydney Road gridlock, my side window quickly misted over. I rubbed the ball of my palm against the glass and peered through the porthole.

My father had not moved. He had managed to button his jacket and looked strangely content with himself as he continued to be battered by the wind and rain. The dog was not content at all. It hung its head and closed its eyes, in a vain attempt to keep the weather out.

I tooted the car horn again and called out to him. My father looked my way and raised an arm in the air as he finally recognised me. Just as he waved to me the traffic suddenly cleared — in both directions. He moved to the edge of the footpath. With his arm outstretched in his red coat, along with the beard and the hair, he looked like Moses about to part the Red Sea.

I took advantage of the break in the traffic, did a U-turn across the tram-tracks, and pulled into the kerb, expecting that he would run for the shelter of my car. But he didn't move. As I watched him through the rear-view mirror he put his hands in his pockets and looked up at the sky. I jumped out of the car and ran for the cover of the verandah above a hairdressing salon just a few feet away from where he and the poor dog were standing.

'Dad, get out of the rain. You'll get pneumonia.'

He shuffled over to me and the dog skipped along next to him, wagging its tail, obviously pleased to be out of the rain. It moved between my legs and sniffed at my shoes while my father glanced across the road to where I had just come from. Although I hadn't seen him in more than six months, he didn't bother saying hello. And neither did I.

'What were you doing over there?' he asked, lifting his chin.

'Laura was tested for new glasses last week. I just picked them up for her.'

'Over there at the eye doctor? It's a bit out of your way, isn't it, this side of town? What'd you pay for them? A fair whack, I'd reckon. Look at that velvet couch there, in the front window. What's an eye doctor need a velvet couch for? It's not like he's a psychiatrist. To tart the place up to match the bill, I bet. You would have paid a fortune.'

I felt a familiar dull pain above my right eye. I suffered from migraines, brought on by stress. His questions were not helpful.

'I don't how much they cost, Dad. Laura wrote a cheque for them. I just handed it over and picked up the glasses.'

'You would have got a receipt. You could check that.'

He raised his eyebrows at me. It was the look he had been giving me for as long as I could remember.

The dog looked up at him and let out a short yelp. He bent down and tickled it under its chin.

'Good girl, good girl,' he repeated, as he patted the dog along its thick, wire-haired coat. The dog poked out an obliging tongue and licked his hand. My father continued to give his attention to the dog as he spoke to me.

'You know you can get a decent pair of glasses for a few dollars at the Salvos, just up the road from here. They've got a bin full of them, just inside the front door. It's a bit of a lucky dip but, if you dig through the bin long enough, you'll find a pair to suit. Does me fine.'

He stood up and, as if to demonstrate, dug a hand into a pocket of the red coat, pulled out a pair of glasses and put them on.

'I got these for five dollars. Beauties.' He smiled at me. 'What do you think?'

The heavy black frames he was wearing were obviously too big for his head while the lenses were so heavily smudged with grime and dirt I wondered how he could see out of them at all.

'You could clean them, I guess,' I answered, before thinking that I might offend him.

He seemed to ignore what I'd said and bent down

again to pick up the dog. It sniffed at him and then nuzzled into the armpit of his coat as he tickled it behind the ear and gently teased it.

'What you need is a coat of your own, don't you, Girlie. A winter coat of your own.'

I shuffled from toe to toe, trying to remain warm while he smooched the dog around the ears.

'What's her name?' I asked. Not that I was interested in the dog but because I could think of nothing else to say to him.

'Girlie. Just Girlie, I call her.'

'Where'd you get her?'

'Well, I was walking home from the TAB one afternoon and she started trailing after me. Followed me all the way home. I gave her a drink of water and a bit of cold sausage, cooked of course. I told her to go home but she wouldn't. She sat on the front doorstep all night and was still out there the next morning. I did the right thing and put a note in the shop window. No one bothered to claim her and she's been with me since.'

He put the dog back down on the footpath. We stood alongside each other, about half a metre apart, staring vacantly into the heavy rain. I coughed nervously as I tried thinking of something to say to him. Talking to my father had always been difficult for me.

'You still having a bet, then? Listening to the races?'

'I *was* listening to the races. My old radio, it fell off the top of the refrigerator a few weeks back. The casing cracked open, split across the back, and a couple of the knobs fell off. I tried putting it back together with electrical tape but couldn't get it working. Haven't been able to listen to a race since.'

'You should have let me know. I've got a spare one at home.'

'How could I have let you know? I haven't seen you in ages.'

Whether he was trying to make me feel guilty or not, I did.

We both continued to look straight ahead, observing the ongoing battle between the traffic and the weather. After a minute, I leaned across to him and tapped him on the shoulder.

'Dad. I've got a CD player with a radio in it. It's in the garage at home. No one uses it. I could bring it over to your place.'

He took off the cheap glasses and put them back in his pocket.

'A CD player?' he smiled. He seemed interested. 'When could you bring it over? I really miss the races. I get down to the TAB a bit but it gives me the shits. Anytime I have a win there's always someone hanging around to put the bite on. When could you come over with it?'

'Well,' I hesitated, 'what about this Saturday?'

'Not Saturday,' he frowned. 'I've got a friend. I spend Saturday nights over at her place. She cooks a roast for the two of us. And Girlie here gets the bone,' he winked. 'I don't get back to my place until Sunday afternoon, about five.'

*Her.* I didn't want to know any more about who she might be, or the details of the friendship he might have with her.

'That's okay. I can come over on Sunday, then. I'll make it about six, to be sure that you're home.'

He leaned across, slapped me hard between the shoulders and ran his hand roughly through my hair as he let out a laugh. Unused to such familiarity, I took a step back and looked at him. He was smiling.

'Good then. Sunday it is.'

I was about to get back in the car when I stopped and looked up at the heavy sky. I turned back to him.

'Let me give you a lift home, so your arse doesn't get any wetter.'

'Na. That's okay.'

'But you'll get wet. You and the dog, both.'

'Yeah, I know. But this rain, it doesn't come often enough these days. I'm enjoying it.'


When the following Sunday arrived I realised I would have a problem if I was to keep my promise to my father. I told my wife, Laura, what I planned to do later that day while we were at the table, eating breakfast. She looked at me over the top of the newspaper she was reading.

'But Justin's got that basketball tournament, the round robin. It's way out in the eastern suburbs somewhere. We were there until late last year. Remember?'

I'd forgotten. Keeping up with the organised activities of my two boys, Justin and Ben, required a full-time social secretary.

'That's okay. We can drop the CD player off at dad's place on the way out. I've just got to show him how it works. It'll only take a few minutes.'

She put the newspaper down on the table and frowned at me.

'We can't do that. It's a bit of a detour and I don't want Justin getting anxious that he might be late. You know what he's like. He's always off his game when he gets worried. Look, I'll take him on my own. You keep Ben with you. Use the sedan and I'll take the wagon.'

'Ben could go to the basketball with you,' I suggested, lamely. 'If I take him with me, he'll get tired. I might be late. He's got school tomorrow.'

'He could come with me,' she offered. 'But you know how he is. He'll end up bored. He drove us mad last year. Remember? Anyway, I'll be later than you. It's a good reason to keep him home.'

While I wasn't happy with Laura's plan I couldn't be bothered arguing with her. She was the organiser in the family and she enjoyed organising me. Ben, our seven-year-old, preferred his mother's company and I immediately imagined him sulking once he'd worked out that he would be spending the whole day and half the night with me.

As soon as Laura and Justin were gone I searched

the house for Ben. He was in Justin's bedroom, sitting on the unmade bed, in his pyjamas. He had a half-eaten piece of vegemite toast hanging out of his mouth as he concentrated on the computer game he was playing. When I was finally able to get his attention we made a deal that I would take him to the pool for a swim and let him have hot chips for lunch on the way home, as long as he was happy to come out with me later on in the day.

'Where to?' he asked, looking at me suspiciously.

'I can't tell you. It's a surprise.'

A good surprise?

'Yes. A good surprise.'

While he seemed pleased, he continued to negotiate.

'Okay then. But can I play the computer again after the swim and before the surprise? Justin said I could play the computer all day, while he was at basketball.'

Ben chose the back seat of the car on the way home from the pool. When I turned and asked him if he'd enjoyed his swim he ignored me and concentrated on the brown paper bag of hot chips, soaked in vinegar and salt. It was never easy for me to get a word out of Ben. He liked to be around his mother, or trailing behind Justin, who he adored. I was sure that he saw me as some kind of puzzle he couldn't solve.

After we got home he played upstairs on the

computer while I did some work in the back garden until around five o'clock. It was time to drive to my father's one-bedroom flat.

I stood in the doorway of Justin's bedroom.

'Come on, Benny, we have to go now.'

He didn't take his eyes off the screen.

'Not yet, Dad. I'm on level six. It's a record for me.'

'Bad luck. Come on. You have to leave that. We made a deal.'

'But I don't want to. I'm still playing.'

I raised my voice a little in an attempt to get him to take my request seriously.

'You're not playing. We're going now, or we'll be late.'

I grabbed the console out of his hands and put it on Justin's desk.

'We're going. Now.'

I offered Ben a seat alongside me in the front of the car but, again, he sat in the back, ignoring my attempts to start a conversation.

'Do you know where we're going, Benny?'

No answer.

'Do you want to know? I bet you can't guess.'

I looked at his sullen face in the rear-view mirror. He looked in no mood to play guessing games.

When we stopped at an intersection I turned around to him. He appeared to be deep in conversation with the action doll he had brought along with him.

'Are you going to talk to me or not?' I demanded.

He shook his head vigorously from side to side.

'Suit yourself, then, Ben. Me neither. I'm not talking to you. See how you like it.'

We pulled up in the street out front of the block of flats where my father lived. I got out of the car and tried breaking the standoff, one more time.

'Ben, do you know who lives here?'

Again, he refused to answer me. Not that I could have expected him to know where he was. I couldn't remember the last time I had brought him here, if at all, and as far as I could recall he had not seen his grandfather in over two years, when we'd had Christmas lunch together at a hotel in the city.

I had to knock at the door of the flat several times before my father answered. When he finally opened the door he looked like he had stumbled out of bed rather than just arrived home. He was still wearing the red coat. It was creased and covered in balls of white fluff. His thick head of white hair was standing on end.

He ignored me completely but smiled with genuine surprise at Ben. I was sure he would be frightened by the dishevelled man standing in front of him but Ben just stared up at his grandfather's imposing presence, from his red coat up to his white beard and wild hair. They stood there, gazing silently at each other, until Ben leaned forward and tugged at his hand.

'You look like Father Christmas. Are you Father Christmas?'

My father chuckled, 'No, not Father Christmas. I'm your grandfather.'

Ben squinted one eye as tightly as he could, tilted his head to one side and inspected his grandfather a little more closely.

'Are you? I thought you were dead.'

'Ben,' I yelled, at the same time as my father burst into laughter. 'Don't say that to your grandfather.' I turned to my father and apologised. 'That's on his mother's side. You know, Laura's dad passed away a few years ago.'

'That's all right,' he laughed again, as he patted Ben gently on the head. 'I'll be dead soon enough. You're just making an early announcement, aren't you, boy?'

I looked at my father, and was surprised by the sparkle in his eyes. I could not remember seeing him so happy.

The dog, Girlie, ran out of the flat, stood on the doorstep for a moment, barked at Ben and then spun around, showing her arse to him and ran back inside. Ben's eyes lit up.

'Can I play with the dog?'

'Of course you can,' my father said, 'but only if you can catch her.'

While Ben chased the dog around the lounge room I set up the CD player on the kitchen bench next to the toaster.

'The volume's here. AM/FM you change with the flick of this switch on the top there. And if you want to use the CD you press this button.'

He watched me closely as I went through the options.

'There's not much to it, Dad,' I added.

'Yeah, I can see that. But don't worry about the CDs or FM. Just turn it to the racing station for me. I'll leave it there.'

Ben was standing in the doorway watching us. He was holding a video case in his hand.

'What is this? Is it a kid's movie? Can I watch it?'

He handed the case to my father, who read the jacket.

'*Harvey*. This is my favourite film, Ben, with one of my favourite actors in it. James Stewart. It's a kid's movie. Well, a family movie, really.'

Ben rubbed his eyes with the palms of his hands. He looked tired.

'What's it about?'

'Well. It's about this man who has a friend called Harvey, who is a rabbit. A giant rabbit.'

'A giant rabbit? Can I watch it?'

'Sure you can. We can all watch it, if you like? Come on, I'll put it on.'

'Dad,' I interrupted. 'I don't know. He's been swimming and he's tired. I've go to get him home to bed. He'll watch for about five minutes and then fall asleep. If he doesn't, he'll get restless. He's into computer games, not old black and white movies.'

My protest trailed off as Ben and my father left the kitchen for the lounge room. I was left alone in the kitchen. I walked over to the window above the sink and looking out into a laneway behind the block of flats.

Across the laneway I could see an elderly woman and man in a backyard, working together in the near darkness. She was standing on a small stepladder picking figs from a tree and handing them down to the man. He carefully placed each fig in a plastic tub he was nursing in his arms. When she had finished picking the figs the woman got down from the ladder and planted a kiss on the man's bald head.

As I watched them my father came back into the kitchen and put the kettle on the stove.

'The movie's on. I'll make us a cuppa. Come on,' he winked at me, 'watch it with us.'

'Okay. I'll make the tea for us. You go and sit down with Ben. How do you have it, again? White with one?'

I carried the two cups of tea into the lounge room. Ben was sitting between Girlie and his grandfather on a battered couch against the wall. I squeezed down besides Ben and passed a cup of tea to my father.

He took the cup out of my hands, nodding at me.

'You'd remember this one, don't you?'

'No, I don't, Dad. I've heard of it but I haven't seen it before.'

'Yes, you have. I took you to see it one night. It was showing with an old Marx Brothers' film. About halfway through *Harvey* you started crying.'

'I don't remember that. Why was I crying? Was I afraid of something? I thought it was supposed to be a comedy.'

'It is. It's a pisser. No, you were crying because you couldn't see the rabbit. You kept poking me and asking, 'Where's the rabbit, Dad? I can't see the rabbit that the man is talking to.' And then you burst into tears. The people around us were looking at you.'

'Did I? And what did you do? Whack me, I suppose, to shut me up.'

He looked at me, deeply offended.

'Of course I didn't whack you. I put you on my knee and cuddled you until you stopped.'

'Shoosh, I can't hear,' Ben interrupted.

I looked along the couch to my father. The light from the television set reflected off his face and hair, which had turned to silver.

I turned to the TV and the scene in a bar. The James Stewart character was ordering two martinis, one for himself and the other for the invisible rabbit. Ben leaned forward and searched the screen.

'Where is he, Grandad, the rabbit? I can't see him.'

'There he is.' My father pointed in the general direction of the TV. 'Just there. He's standing inside the door, near that other fella. You've got to look close, Ben. You tell me when you've spotted him.'

Ben's eyes got heavier and his body began to lean to one side, into my father. The dog got up, to save itself from being pinned between them, and jumped onto my father's lap. Ben shifted a little closer and rested his head against my father's shoulder.

'Can you see the rabbit?' my father asked him.

'Yeah. I can see him,' Ben drawled as he his eyes closed. 'The rabbit.'

# Acknowledgements

For Erin, Siobhan, Drew, Grace and Nina, we know from *Nebraska* that 'nothing feels better than blood on blood'.

For Sara, aren't I the lucky boy then?

For Bev Healy (1939–2009), you gave us the story of the bird who never forgets. We miss you.

For Chris and Bronwyn, you have shown us courage. For Indigo, out of the ashes comes a story.

For the occasional philosophers and dear friends — Chris, Mammad, Sevgi, Tom, Foley, Justin, George, Paul, Arnold, Damien, Robbie, Stephen, Sab, Dennis, John, Oxford Sean and Freo Sean — I thank you for your generosity.

And finally, for my family, the crazy gang — Dawn, Philip, Brian, Deborah, Wayne, Tracey, and all the kids and hangers-on — I love you.

The lyrics reproduced in the epigraph on page *vii* are from the song *My Father's House* (© Bruce Springsteen, ASCAP) from the album *Nebraska* by Bruce Springsteen.